THE GUNSMITH

461

Standoff in Labyrinth

THE GUNSMITH

461

Standoff in Labyrinth

J.R. Roberts

SPEAKING VOLUMES, LLC
NAPLES, FLORIDA
2020

Standoff in Labyrinth

ISBN 978-1-64540-278-7

Chapter One

Labyrinth, Texas was growing by leaps and bounds, and Rick Hartman had always intended his Rick's Place to be at the center of it. But lately a new faction had risen to power, starting with the election of the mayor, Ted Buchanan, who had even convinced Rick to vote for him. But in the months since his election, he had turned his back on most of the campaign promises he'd made. In doing so, he had made an enemy of Rick Hartman, who was considering running against him in the next election, which was over a year away . . .

***

Rick rolled over in bed, bumping hips with his latest paramour, Ruth Bridges. He usually picked a girl from the staff of his saloon and casino, Rick's Place, but a few months earlier he had met Ruth when she moved to town and opened a dress shop.

"Are you really thinking of running for mayor?" she'd asked him, the night before.

"Are you really considering bringing Paris fashions to South Texas?" he'd asked.

"Hey," she said, "that could be a good thing. But what good do you think could possibly come from Rick Hartman becoming a politician?"

Sex had ensued and discontinued that discussion . . .

Now it was the next morning, and he stared at the twin melons that were her tidy little butt. She was lying on her belly with her head turned away from him, her honey-colored hair fanned out on the pillow.

"If you wanted to wake me up," she said, "you could have figured another way, other than bumping me."

"Sorry," he said, "I'm still not used to sleeping with somebody."

She turned her head to look at him.

"So you really don't let your bed partners sleep here?"

"No," he said, "they go back to their own rooms."

"What makes me different?"

"Well," he said, "you don't have a room in this building, and I don't want to make you walk across town."

"I appreciate that, sir," she said, reaching over to run her hand down his nude body. "What can I do to show you how much?"

"Well, for one, you can roll over," he said.

"You don't like my ass?" she asked. She moved her hand from his body to her own, fondling her ass cheeks.

"I love both your back side," he said, "and your front side."

"Show me."

He laughed, rolled toward her and began to run his tongue down her back. When he reached her ass, he kissed each cheek, then spread them and probed with his tongue.

She leaped up as if electrocuted and asked, "What the hell are you doin'?"

"You asked me to prove it," he said.

"I didn't ask you to stick your tongue up my asshole!" she scolded. "Where'd you learn that, from some whore?"

"French whore, actually," he said.

"Well, I didn't like it," she said. "And don't think I'll ever do the same to you. You got that?"

"I got it," he said. He moved in for a kiss and she held her hand in front of her face.

"Don't think I'm gonna kiss you after you stuck your tongue up my ass!"

He leaned the other way, grabbed an open bottle of whiskey from the night table, and took a healthy swig.

"How's that?" he asked.

This time when he leaned in for a kiss, she accommodated him. Holding her in his arms he kissed her deeply, at the same time taking her down onto her back.

He kissed her neck, her shoulders, her hard little breasts. This girl did not have an ounce of fat on her, which was just the way Rick liked his women. He found women built that way could go all night, and Ruth was a perfect example of that. She may not have liked his tongue up her ass, but that was the only thing about sex she didn't like.

He kissed his way down between her legs, where he found her pussy hot and wet when he pressed his mouth and face to it.

"Now how come you don't mind me putting my mouth here?" he asked, looking up at her from between her spread thighs.

"Never you mind," she said. "You just stop talkin' and put that tongue of yours to work."

"Yes, Ma'am," he said, and bent to his extremely pleasant task.

Chapter Two

The three men met in a dark, back room.

"Close the door," the first man said to the Third as he arrived.

The Third man closed the door tightly, then joined the First and Second man at the table.

"This is a private meeting," First said. "No one outside this room is to know what we discuss. Is that understood all of us?"

Both of the other men nodded.

"Where do we stand on Rick Hartman?" First asked.

"He's been a pillar of this community for years," Second said.

"But we believe the community has outgrown him," Third said. "For a long time he was the only game in town, but that's no longer the case. There are other saloons and gambling establishments in town."

"So he's not the big cat in Labyrinth, anymore," First said.

"But he wants to be," Second said. "He's not ready to step down. In fact, what if he's thinking of running for mayor next election."

"And if he did?" First asked.

"He'd probably win," Third said.

"And we can't have that," First said, "can we?"

"So what do we do?" Third asked.

"Kill 'im?" Second asked.

"That would be stupid," First said. "We don't want to make him a martyr. Besides, we're not criminals."

"So what are you suggestin'?" Third asked.

First looked at Second and Third.

"I suggest we change his image," First said.

Second and Third looked at each other, then back at First.

"So who do we have him kill?" Second asked.

***

Rick came down from his rooms above Rick's Place, saw his bartender, Shiloh, wiping down the bar, getting ready for the day.

"'mornin', boss," the young man greeted him. "Coffee?"

"Definitely," Rick said, going to his table.

Shiloh brought him a pot and a mug, poured the coffee.

"Breakfast?"

"Ham-and-eggs," Rick said. "Thanks."

"Comin' up."

The only time Shiloh cooked was at breakfast. Rick's Place actually didn't serve food, except for occasionally putting out a jar of hardboiled eggs.

When Shiloh came back with a plate of ham-and-eggs, he also had a note.

"Somebody left this in the kitchen for you, boss," he said.

"Thanks, Shy."

Rick took the paper, set it down next to his plate and started to eat. A note slipped into the kitchen couldn't be anything good. But he knew this new faction in town was plotting against him. He had heard the whispers. With other saloons and gambling halls opening in Labyrinth, and the town growing, he either had to step up and try to take a central role or leave town and start over somewhere else.

Halfway through his breakfast, he picked up the folded piece of paper and read it.

Shiloh came over, traded a full pot of coffee for the empty one.

"Bad news, boss?" he asked.

"That depends, Shiloh," Rick said. "That depends."

***

The note told him that somebody was planning a move against him, and if he wanted to know who, he should be at the stockyards at midnight, alone.

It took him all day to decide to go ahead and be there. At quarter to midnight, he stuck a gun in his belt and told Shiloh to get somebody to cover for him.

"What's goin' on, boss?" Shiloh asked.

"I need a little backup, if you're up for it."

"Whatever you say, boss."

"Grab that shotgun from beneath the bar and meet me out front," Rick said.

When the young bartender came through the batwing doors with the shotgun, Rick led the way towards the stockyards.

They were almost there when Rick called a halt to their progress.

"This is as far as you go, kid," he told Shiloh. "Just stay alert."

"Are you sure, boss?" Shiloh asked. "I can get closer."

"Like I said," Rick repeated, "just stay alert."

"Whatever you say."

Rick walked the rest of the way to the stockyards, eyes and ears alert. When he got there, he waited just over an hour, but nobody showed. He finally walked back to where he had left the young bartender.

"You see or hear anything?" he asked.

"No, sir," Shiloh said. "What happened?"

"Nobody showed."

"Whataya wanna do?" Shiloh asked.

"Let's head back to the saloon," Rick said. "And—"

"—I know," the young man interrupted him. "Be alert."

Chapter Three

When Clint Adams received the telegram from Rick Hartman saying he needed help, he dropped what he was doing and headed for Labyrinth, Texas.

He rode into town a week after receiving the telegram. Each of his last few visits began with the same feeling in the pit of his stomach. Once a small town which was a good place for him to relax, clear his head and take a breath, Labyrinth was growing by leaps and bounds. It would soon reach the point where he'd need to find himself a new place to relax.

But he certainly wasn't there to take it easy now. The tone of Rick's telegram said he had a real problem, and Rick usually handled those kinds of things himself. But at least this time Clint Adams was responding to a call for help from one of his close friends.

He rode Eclipse directly to Rick's Place, arriving late in the afternoon when business was usually picking up. Leaving the Darley outside, standing free as usual with his reins dangling, Clint went in and stopped just inside the batwing doors. Everything appeared normal: the gaming tables were in full swing, and there was hardly any elbow room at the bar. Yet, the longer he stood there and watched, the more he felt that things were *not* normal.

Clint knew the bartender, Shiloh, and since he didn't see Rick at his usual table, he walked to the bar. Many of the customers recognized him from previous visits and moved aside to give him room. He waved and Shiloh spotted him right away.

"Jail," the young man said, as he came over.

"What?"

"Rick's in jail."

"What for?"

"Murder."

"What the hell—why didn't he say so in his telegram?" Clint asked.

"He wasn't in jail when he sent the telegram, and since they put him there, he hasn't had a chance to send another one. Plus, he figured you were on your way, anyhow."

"All right," Clint said. "Give me a beer and I'll get over there and find out what the hell is going on."

Shiloh set him up with a mug, which he drank down quickly to get rid of the trail dust, and then headed for the jail.

***

Clint usually had very little to do with the law in Labyrinth. It was generally known that when he was there, he

11

wasn't looking for trouble. He wasn't even sure he knew the sheriff's name.

As he entered the jailhouse, he became dead sure he didn't know the man seated behind the desk. He'd never seen him before.

"Sheriff?"

"Can I help you?" The man was in his forties, with steel grey eyes and a deep, bass voice. There was also a no-nonsense demeanor about him, even seated.

"I'd like to see your prisoner."

"Which one?"

"How many do you have?"

"Two," the lawman said. "One's in for drunk and disorderly, the other one for murder."

"The one who's in for murder," Clint said. "Rick Hartman, right?"

"You ain't his lawyer."

"No, I'm not."

"Then why should I let you see him?"

"I'm his friend."

"Still not a good enough reason," the man said. "Who are you?"

"My name's Clint Adams."

"Ah, the Gunsmith," the man said. "I heard you came to town from time to time. Just passin' through?"

"No, I'm here to find out what the hell is going on. Tell me, how long have you been sheriff? I've never seen you before."

"The name's Ritter, Sheriff Vince Ritter," the man said, "and I've been wearin' the badge for two months. When's the last time you were here?"

"Probably three months ago."

"All right, that explains why we've never seen each other," Ritter said. "Now tell me why I should let you see him?"

"Because there's no reason not to."

Ritter actually smiled.

"I like that," he said. "I'll need your gun."

"That's going to be a problem," Clint said.

"I know a man like you doesn't like to give it up, but I can't let you go in there with a gun. If you want to see your friend, you'll have to give it up."

Clint hesitated, then figured Rick's arrest wasn't just a ploy to get his gun away from him. He drew it from his holster and handed it to the man, butt first. Ritter opened his top drawer and put it inside, then grabbed his keys.

"Let's go," he said.

Clint followed the tall man to the cell block, waited while he unlocked the main door.

Chapter Four

"What the hell—" Clint started, then turned his head and looked at the sheriff.

"I'll give you two some privacy," Ritter said, and withdrew.

Rick stood up from the cot and walked to the bars.

"Thanks for coming," he said.

"As quick as I could," Clint said, "but it doesn't look like that was quick enough to keep you out of trouble."

"Oh, I was in trouble already," Rick said, "but it got worse."

"Shiloh told me you were in here for murder?"

"That's the worst part."

His friend looked more disheveled than Clint had ever seen him. Always well groomed, being in jail had wrung him out.

"What the hell's been going on, Rick?"

"There are some new people in town, new businesses, a new mayor . . . they're all anxious to get rid of me."

"Get rid of . . .? You mean . . . kill?"

"I didn't think so," Rick said. "At least, not me."

"Who did they kill, Rick?" Clint asked.

"I've been seeing a woman, she has a business here in town, a dress shop. Her name is—was—Ruth Bridges."

"Was?"

"I got a note at my place, told me somebody was plotting against me, and if I wanted more information to be at the stockyards at midnight."

"So you went?"

"I did," Rick said. "I had Shiloh cover me."

"And?"

"I waited an hour, nobody showed up. So we went back to my place. Shiloh got back behind the bar. I went up to my rooms, and . . . Ruth was there. She was in my bed, with her throat cut. There was blood . . . everywhere."

"And?"

"I froze. Then there was pounding on the door, and it was the sheriff."

"He arrested you?"

"Not right then. He questioned me, had the body removed, told me not to leave town—as if I would." Rick never left town. "It was a couple of days later that he arrested me, after I sent you the telegram."

"And you've been in here since?" Clint asked.

"Yes."

"Is there going to be a trial?" Clint asked. "Do you have a lawyer?"

"I have a lawyer," Rick said. "No trial date has been set."

"Why not?"

"I don't know."

"Who's your lawyer?"

"A local guy named Judd," Rick said. "Raymond Judd."

"Did you hire him?"

"No," Rick said, "he just walked in here to see me, offered his services."

"Can you trust him?"

"I don't know who I can trust," Rick said. "That's why I sent you the telegram. I knew I'd end up needing somebody I could trust."

"Well, you've got him," Clint said. "I'll get you out of here. I can send for Talbot Roper."

"No," Rick said. "I just need you."

"He's the best detective in the business."

"How long would it take him to get here from Denver?" Rick asked. "If he's even in Denver, right now."

"I'll check," Clint said. "Meanwhile, I'll go and see your lawyer. I'm going to get you out of here."

"You're not thinking of breaking me out, are you?" Rick asked.

"Only if it comes to that," Clint said. "I certainly wouldn't let you hang for a murder you didn't commit."

"How do you know I didn't commit it?" Rick asked.

"Because I know you," Clint said.

"See?" Rick said. "I knew I could trust you."

"I'll be in touch."

He left the cell block, went back to Sheriff Ritter's desk. The man opened his drawer, took out Clint's gun and set it on the desk.

"You get what you wanted?" Ritter asked.

"Not by a longshot," Clint replied. "I want to know how you knew to go to Rick's room that night."

"I don't have to tell you that."

"You'll have to tell, eventually," Clint pointed out. "In court."

"I'll deal with that when the time comes."

"How well do you know Judd, the lawyer?"

"I've seen him around."

"Who told him to approach Rick about representing him?" Clint asked.

"I don't—that's not for me to say."

"What *can* you tell me, Sheriff?"

"Nothing," Sheriff Ritter said. "You're not his lawyer, and you don't work for his lawyer."

"We'll see about that," Clint said, and left.

Chapter Five

Clint found the office of Raymond Judd, Attorney-at-Law. It was on a side street which did not seem to be part of Labyrinth's growth. He knocked and when no one called out from inside, he entered. There was a secretary's desk, but no secretary seated at it.

"Hello? Anybody here?"

"Hey, come on in," a man's voice called from another room.

There was an open doorway behind the desk, so Clint went there and entered. A man in his forties smiled from behind his desk and beckoned for Clint to come forward.

"My secretary went on a break and hasn't come back yet," the man said.

"When was that?" Clint asked.

"Several months ago," the man said. "I guess I shouldn't've kept askin' her to sit in my lap when she took a letter." He stood up and extended his hand. "Ray Judd. How can I help you?"

"My name's Clint Adams. I'm a friend of Rick Hartman's."

"I've heard that," Judd said. "When'd you get to town?"

"About an hour ago."

"You don't waste any time," Judd said. "Have a seat." He sat back down behind his desk as Clint also sat. "What can I do for you?"

"Why is Rick Hartman still in jail?"

"That's easy," Judd said. "I can't get him out."

"Why not?"

"The judge is bein' a sonofabitch." This man had a slight Southern accent.

"Does he have something against Rick, or you?"

"It might be both."

"How did you happen to become Rick's lawyer?"

"The judge appointed me."

"Aren't there other lawyers in town?"

"Well, like you said, he may have it in for me and for Hartman. This way it's a package deal."

"There must be a way to get him out until the trial," Clint reasoned.

"I'm still tryin' to come up with one," Judd said.

"What's the judge's name?"

"Judge Jeremiah Wilkie."

"I don't know him."

"He's been here about three months, was appointed to the bench just before that."

"So he's flexing new muscles."

"Indeed."

19

"So we have a fairly new sheriff and a fairly new judge."

"And don't forget a fairly new mayor."

"And you?"

"Toss me in there," Judd said. "I've been here about six months. I know you've been in and out of town during that time, but there hasn't been a reason for us to cross paths."

"Did you know the victim?"

"No," Judd said, "but she was new to town, also. Labyrinth is changing, Mr. Adams."

"I'm seeing that, Mr. Judd. What are you doing to find out who really killed the woman?"

"My job is to defend Mr. Hartman against the charges," Judd pointed out, "not play detective and find out who killed her."

"But wouldn't that be helpful in his defense?"

"It definitely would," Judd said.

"Okay, then," Clint said, "hire me to find out."

"Uh, I actually don't have the funds to hire a detective—"

"Give me a dollar."

Judd looked pleased with that idea.

"Excellent suggestion," he said, and handed Clint a dollar.

Clint stood up.

"Where will you start?" Judd asked.

"She must've had friends in town," he said. "But before I look for them, I'm going to talk to the judge."

"Well," Judd said, "that should be an interestin' meetin'. Why not come back here later, and you can tell me about it over supper?"

"That's a deal," Clint said. "I'll be here at seven."

"See you then."

Clint left Judd's office and headed for the courthouse.

***

The City Hall and courthouse building was new, a pristine Three-story brick structure. Labyrinth really was becoming a place Clint would not want to spend his leisure time. All they would have to do to top it off was install a new and modern police department. Clint's preference for law enforcement still ran to sheriffs and marshals.

He entered the building, discovered that the courtrooms were on the first floor, the judge's chamber the second, and the mayor's office the third. He mounted the steps to the second floor and found a door marked Judge's Chambers. As he entered, a young, sad-eyed man looked up at him from a desk.

"Can I help you?"

"I assume you're Judge Wilkie's clerk?"

"I have that privilege."

"I'd like to see him."

"Do you have an appointment?"

"I don't," Clint said. "I only just got to town. Up to an hour ago I didn't know who Judge Wilkie was."

"I see," the clerk said. "And what do you wish to speak to the judge about?"

"Rick Hartman."

"Ah," the clerk said. "And you are?"

"Clint Adams."

The young man recognized the name, but he tried to seem unimpressed. He stood up and said, "I'll tell the judge you're here. Do you have any, uh, legal standing?"

"I'm Rick Hartman's friend," Clint said, "but I know what you mean. I'm working for his lawyer, Mr. Judd."

"I see," the clerk said. "Please wait here."

The clerk went through the door to the judge's chamber and returned in seconds.

"The Judge has agreed to give you ten minutes," he said to Clint.

"Well, that should be enough," Clint said. "Thanks."

He circled the clerk's desk and went through the doorway as the clerk held it open for him.

Chapter Six

"Mr. Adams," the fairly young judge greeted. "Have a seat."

Clint was used to judges being older gentleman who have worked long and hard to get to the bench. This man seemed barely fifty, with a full head of black hair and a well-cared for mustache. He did not offer to shake hands.

"Your clerk said ten minutes," Clint said. "I think I'll stand for that time."

"My clerk takes liberties," Judge Wilkie said. "Please, sit and we'll talk. Don't worry about the time."

"Thank you, Judge," Clint said, and sat.

"Now," the Judge said, seating himself, "what can I do for you? My clerk tells me you're Rick Hartman's friend, but that you're also working for his lawyer. Are you a detective as well as the Gunsmith?"

"Much to Allan Pinkerton's dismay, I've turned him down several times when he's offered me a job, but I can't say I'm a detective. I do have some experience in that area, though."

"I don't know Mr. Pinkerton, but I'm an admirer of his. He must have a high opinion of your abilities."

"I worked for him during the war," Clint said. "That was enough."

"I see," Wilkie said. "You must've been very young."

"We all got a lot older, during that war," Clint said.

"Indeed we did."

"Judge, I'm wondering why Rick Hartman is still in jail?" Clint said.

"He's under arrest for murder, Mr. Adams."

"Without bail?"

"I don't believe bail is warranted, in this instance," Wilkie said. "Not when the charge is first degree murder."

"But wouldn't the final decision be up to you?"

"Yes, it is."

"And wouldn't Rick be able to mount a better defense if he was out of jail and able to work with his lawyer?"

"It seems to me you and Mr. Judd should be very capable of doing that while he's in jail," the Judge said. "I mean, what if I let him out and he lights out for parts unknown?"

"Rick's a businessman," Clint said. "He wouldn't just leave."

"Not even to avoid a murder charge?"

"He's not guilty."

"That's going to be for a jury to decide," Judge Wilkie said. "And that's another reason why he's still in a cell. I have to get a jury together."

"A jury of twelve impartial people."

"Hard to get," Wilkie said. "He's lived here a long time. People know him."

"Yes, they do."

"But he doesn't have many friends, it seems," Wilkie said. "Acquaintances, customers, but not many friends. That must be why he sent for you."

Clint stood up.

"Thanks for seeing me, Judge."

Clint started to leave the office, stopped and turned when the Judge spoke again.

"Where are you going now?"

"To find out who killed Ruth Bridges."

"Did you know her?"

"No, I never heard of her until I got to town," Clint answered.

"How do you expect to find out who killed her?" Wilkie asked.

"By asking questions," Clint said. "That's about the only thing I can think to do."

"Questions of who?"

"Well, Rick may not have many friends in town," Clint said, "but I'm hoping Ruth did."

Chapter Seven

"You think of somethin' you didn't ask Hartman?" the Sheriff asked, as Clint reentered his office.

"Just one thing," Clint said. "I just came from seeing Judge Wilkie."

"And he says it's all right for you to see the prisoner?"

"He does."

Ritter shrugged.

"Then it's all right with me. Gun."

Clint handed it over again, then followed the lawman to the cell block.

"What's going on?" Rick asked, as Ritter left the block.

"How many friends did Ruth have, Rick?" Clint asked.

"I don't know," he said. "A few, I guess. You'd have to ask Lily."

"Who's Lily?"

"She works in Ruth's store," Rick said. "I'm guessing she'd know who Ruth's friends were."

"You never met any of them?"

"Ruth and I didn't spend much time outside, if you know what I mean."

"I do," Clint said. "I'll get back to you."

"Hey, wait," Rick said. "Did you see Judd?"

"And the judge," Clint said. "I'm still working on getting you out."

"Make sure my place is all right," Rick said. "Tell them to stay open. I'm going to need money to pay for my defense, I'm sure."

"At least a dollar, so far," Clint said, and left before Rick could ask what he meant.

***

Clint wanted to find Ruth Bridges' shop, but he needed to get Eclipse boarded at a livery stable, and then something in his own stomach.

He got Eclipse taken care of, then decided to go and see Lily before eating. He wanted to make sure the dress shop was still open.

As he entered, a bell above the door announced his arrival. A dark-haired young woman was helping a faded, middle-aged lady, and held up a finger to him, as if to say she'd be right there.

He looked around but couldn't even pretend to be interested in the inventory, so he just waited.

After the young woman escorted the older one to the door, she turned and looked at Clint. She was slim, with a pretty face and long, dark hair. She looked to be in her early twenties.

"We don't get too many men coming in here alone," she admitted. "Are you looking for something for your wife?"

"No," he said, "are you Lily?"

"I am."

"My name is Clint Adams," he said. "I'm here to ask you some questions about Ruth Bridges."

Her face fell.

"Ruth's dead. Did you not know that?"

"I do know that," he said. "I'm trying to find out who killed her."

Now she frowned.

"They arrested Rick Hartman."

"He didn't kill her."

"How do you know?"

"Because he told me he didn't, and I believe him."

"You're his friend," she said. "I've heard that."

"I am his friend, but I'm also working for his lawyer, Mr. Judd."

"I don't know him." She turned and walked around behind the counter, to put it between her and Clint. "What can I possibly do for you?"

"I'd like to find out who Ruth's friends were."

"Do you think one of her friends killed her?" she asked.

"I'd like to talk to her friends, see if they know anything about Ruth possibly being threatened, or simply being afraid of somebody."

"Well, she never said anything to me," Lily said. "Ruth was a happy person."

"No problems?"

"I didn't like the relationship she had with Mr. Hartman," Lily said. "He wasn't the kind of man she should have been involved with."

"Why not?"

"Because she was a lady, and he was . . . well. A gambler. He owned a saloon. I know being with him excited her, but I never thought it was good for her. I guess I was right."

"So you're convinced Rick has something to do with her death."

"I didn't have any reason not to believe he killed her, until you walked in."

"Let's just assume for a minute he didn't."

"Then it was someone connected to him, not her," Lily said.

"A jealous man? Or woman?"

"Could be either one."

"Were there other men in Ruth's life?"

"From time to time," Lily said. "She had men interested in her, but nothing serious."

"What about other women interested in Rick?" Clint asked.

"I wouldn't know anything about that," she said. "Maybe one of his saloon girls was jealous."

"I'll check into that," Clint said. "Meanwhile, can you give me the names of any of her friends?"

"I suppose I could," she said, "but I don't want to get anyone in trouble."

"Like I said," he told her, "I just want to ask some questions. The same kind I've been asking you."

"I—I can write down some names," she said, biting her lip.

"If you want to check me out with the sheriff first, you can do that."

She studied him.

"No," she said, "I suppose you're all right. I've lived here a few years, and I know you come to town from time to time. I've never heard that you caused any trouble."

"Believe me, Lily," he said, "I hate trouble."

He waited while she scribbled down a few names for him, and where they could be found. When Clint accepted it from her and read it, he saw that most of the half dozen were other storekeepers.

"What about this last name?" he asked. "Harlan Kellog?"

"He once asked Ruth to marry him," she said. "She refused."

"Why?"

"He's a rancher," she said. "Ruth said she never wanted to live on a ranch."

"And where's his spread?"

"Just north of town," she said. "It's pretty big. It's called the Bar H."

"All right, Lily," he said, pocketing the list. "Thanks for your help."

"If Mr. Hartman didn't do it, I hope you can help your friend."

"Thanks."

"But if he did it," she added, "I hope they hang him."

Chapter Eight

Clint went to his hotel, where they usually kept a room reserved for him.

"Sorry, sir," said a clerk he'd never seen before, "but that room is not available."

"Then just give me what you've got," Clint said. Labyrinth really was changing. His only reason to keep coming back there in the future would be to see Rick—if he managed to keep his friend from being hanged.

The clerk gave him a room and he carried his saddlebags and rifle to it. It wasn't as large as the one he usually got, but at least it wasn't overlooking the front of the hotel, and there was no access from the window.

He sat for a moment on the bed and studied the list Lily had written out for him. He'd probably start the next day by riding out to the Bar H, then come back to town and start talking to other storeowners.

As the clock approached seven, he left his room and headed for the lawyer's office. Raymond Judd was waiting right out front for him.

"Guess you can tell I'm hungry," he said to Clint. "There's a place just up the street I like."

"Your pick," Clint said. "Lead on."

They started walking.

"How did you make out with Judge Wilkie?"

"I was surprised he was so young," Clint said, "and willing to talk to me. I'm used to men like Judge Parker, who are usually ornery."

"Wilkie's a new breed, all right," Judd said, "but he does have his ornery moments—seems to be usually when I'm in his courtroom."

They came to the place Judd had referred to, a small café called Chino's.

"Mexican?" Clint asked.

"You'd think so, but no. More like a small steak-house."

"Hello, Ray," a stocky man said. He looked like an ex-boxer, with big hands and a scarred face.

"How are you, Chino?"

"Ah, what's the point of complainin'," the man said. "Who's your friend?"

"This is Clint Adams," Judd said. "He's doin' some work for me."

"The Gunsmith, in my place?" Chino said. "That ain't never happened before."

"How long has your place been here?" Clint asked.

"A few years, now," Chino said.

"Well," Clint said, "I don't usually stay very long when I come to town. Sorry I haven't been in."

"Hey, you're here now," Chino said. "Come on, I'll seat'cha in the back."

He sat them and asked if they wanted a couple of mugs of beer.

"Sounds good to me," Judd said.

"I'll go for that."

"And a couple of steaks?" Judd asked Clint.

"Let's do it," Clint said.

"Comin' up, gents," Chino promised.

"So what else did you do today, besides meet with Wilkie?" Judd asked.

"I went back to the jail, talked with Rick again. He sent me to Ruth's dress shop to see a girl who works there named Lily."

"What'd she tell you?"

"Not much, but she gave me a few names of people she thought might know something."

"I wonder if there's anybody I know on that list?" Judd asked.

"Take a look," Clint said, and handed it over.

Judd looked the list over, said, "Oh yeah, I know some of these people."

"I thought I'd start with a visit to the Bar H tomorrow," Clint said. "Lily told me that Harlan Kellog proposed to Ruth once. Maybe he didn't like her keeping company with Rick."

"And these storekeepers are familiar to me," Judd said, handing the list back. "What exactly are you looking for?"

"I'm hoping to find a jealous man," Clint said, "or maybe even a woman."

"Ruth Bridges' throat was cut," Judd said. "You really think a woman would do that?"

"I don't see why not," Clint said, putting the list back in his pocket. "I guess I'll also check with Rick and see if any of these people have something against him."

"You sound like you know what you're doin'," Judd said.

Chino reappeared, carrying a tray laden with the two steak plates, and the two full beer mugs. The stocky man balanced it all expertly and set the table without spilling a drop.

"Enjoy, gents."

They did.

Chapter Nine

Clint offered to pay for supper, but Judd insisted he should pay, since Clint was working for him. But no money changed hands before they left, so Clint assumed Judd had an account there.

Outside Judd said, "Saloon?"

"I don't think so," Clint said. "I've been moving all day. I need to get some sleep so I can get an early start tomorrow."

"All right," Judd said. "You'll let me know what you find out."

"You'll be the first," Clint promised, "even before Rick."

"That's good," Judd said.

"Thanks for supper," Clint said, and they went their separate ways.

In his hotel room Clint started to undress and, totally fatigued, fell asleep only halfway done.

***

The next morning, he awoke very early, having slept for more than ten hours. He washed up, got dressed and went downstairs to the hotel dining room for breakfast.

He didn't know any of the waiters. When he asked one of them who owned the hotel, he found out that it now had a new owner. Just another example of the changes happening in Labyrinth.

After breakfast he walked to the livery, saddled Eclipse and headed for the Bar H Ranch.

***

Upon arrival at the ranch, he found a lot of activity around the corral, where someone was trying to break a wild bronc. He dismounted in front of the two-story house and walked over to the corral in time to see a cowboy thrown.

"All right, who's next to try and break Toby?" someone shouted.

Clint could see why the horse had been named Toby. He was a Tobiano Paint. Tobianos were usually white, with various colored patches on them, and solid faces. The colors were any of the common horse pigments; black, brown or bay. But this one's patches seemed to be red, like the color of a Red Roan. At the moment, the colt was snorting and slamming his front hooves on the ground. This horse was the largest Paint Clint had ever seen.

"Ain't there nobody's gonna take the challenge?" the man yelled.

"What for, boss?" another man called out. "He's already thrown six of us."

"Hey, we got a stranger here," another man shouted, indicating Clint.

The boss, who Clint assumed was either Harlan Kellog, or his foreman, looked at Clint and asked, "What about it, stranger? Whoever breaks him gets a hundred dollars."

"Well," Clint said, "I'll give it a try, but I'll do it my own way."

"How's that?" the man asked.

"You'll see."

Clint turned and whistled. Eclipse came trotting over from the house.

"Wow," the boss said, "that's quite a horse. I'm Tim Crockett, the foreman."

"My name's Clint and this is Eclipse. Can you get that gate?"

"Sure thing."

Crockett opened the gate and Clint walked into the corral with Eclipse. With the Darley in the corral with the white stallion, the men didn't know where to look first.

Clint walked Eclipse over to the Tobiano Paint.

Chapter Ten

Clint spoke briefly into Eclipse's ear, then walked away, leaving the two horses next to each other. The Tobiano was almost as large as Eclipse, but not quite.

Clint stood next to the foreman, while the other men around the corral wondered what he was doing?

"What's goin' on?" Tim Crockett asked.

"Let's give them a few minutes," Clint said. "That colt's a Tobiano Paint, isn't it?"

"It is," Crockett said. "You know your horses. That Eclipse, he's a Darley Arabian, ain't he?"

"You know yours, too," Clint said. "But what's with the red patches?"

"Toby's the product of a Paint sire, but Red Roan dam."

"How did that happen?"

"Believe me, it wasn't deliberate," Crockett said. "A storm knocked down our corral a few years back, and they just . . . found each other. Once it happened, we were real curious what the outcome would be. It was Toby. The red started comin' in last year when he was two."

Clint looked at Crockett. The man was in his late thirties, tall and rangy.

"How long have you been foreman here?" Clint asked.

"A few years," Crockett said "since the longtime foreman died. He worked for my boss twenty years. I was surprised when the boss asked me to take the job."

"He must have a lot of faith in you."

"I hope he does. Hey, what's happenin'?"

The two horses, Eclipse and Toby, had their heads together.

"They're getting acquainted," Clint said.

"You think this'll help break Toby?" Crockett asked.

"It can't hurt."

The cowhands surrounding the corral were starting to get impatient, and then a tall, barrel-chested man in his fifties came walking over from the house.

"What's goin' on, Tim?" he bellowed. "You break that horse, yet?"

"No, sir," Crockett said, "he's thrown six men already. But this stranger had an idea. That's his horse in there with Toby."

"Toby," the man said. "I hate that name."

The man Clint assumed was Harlan Kellog stepped up to the corral for a look.

"That's quite a good-lookin' horse, Mister," he said to Clint. "Darley Arabian?"

"Yes, sir."

"And what's he doin'?"

"He's calming your Tobiano."

"Is he, now?" The man turned and looked at Clint. "I'm Harlan Kellog."

"Clint Adams."

"You're the Gunsmith."

"Yes, sir."

A wave of muttering and comments went through the surrounding cowhands.

"You didn't come here to break my horse."

"No, sir, I didn't know about it until I rode up," Clint said. "I came to talk to you."

"About what?"

"Rick Hartman and Ruth Bridges."

"Yeah," Kellog said, "I heard you were a friend of his. You tryin' to get him off for murderin' Ruth?"

"I am," Clint said. "I don't think he did it."

"Well, I think he did," Kellog said. "Now you can get off my property."

"Can't we just talk?"

"No."

Kellog turned away but stopped when Tim Crockett stepped in and said something in his ear. Kellog turned back.

"I tell you what," he said to Clint. "You break that Tobiano and you can come inside, and we'll talk. If he throws you, you leave."

"Deal," Clint said.

Clint turned and walked to where the two horses still had their heads together. He heard the cowpokes around him making bets on how long it would take him to get thrown.

"Hey, big guy," Clint said to Eclipse. "You get acquainted? Huh?"

"You want somebody to take the Darley?" Crockett called out.

"He's fine," Clint called back. "Aren't you?" He stroked Eclipse's neck, then reached over and stroked Toby's. "And how about you? You doing all right?"

Toby looked at Clint. A ripple went through his neck, but he stood still under Clint's touch.

"All right, then," Clint said, "let's see how this goes."

He moved between the two massive equine bodies. He could feel the heat coming off them.

He put his foot in the stirrup of the saddle on Toby's back, grasped the saddle horn, and pulled himself up.

Eclipse came over and bumped Toby, trapping Clint's leg between them. He waited for the Tobiano to buck, but he didn't. He picked up the reins and urged the Paint into a walk around the corral, with Eclipse right by their side.

42

Standoff in Labyrinth

"Well, I'll be damned," somebody said.

Chapter Eleven

Clint followed Harlan Kellog into his house, with Tim Crockett walking alongside.

"That was the damndest thing I ever saw," the foreman said. "That horse damn near crippled six of our men."

"Then it was time for a new approach," Clint said.

Kellog lead them into a main sitting room which contained an overstuffed divan, some armchairs, and a large desk set in front of a window that looked out over the front of the house. Clint could see the corral.

"Whiskey?" Kellog asked.

"A little early for me," Clint said.

"Coffee, then?"

"No, I'm fine."

"Whiskey, Tim?"

"Not too early for me."

Kellog poured two whiskeys and handed one glass to his foreman, then went to sit behind his desk.

"What do you want to know?" he asked.

"Ruth Bridges," Clint said. "Do you know anybody who wanted to kill her?"

"Yeah, Rick Hartman."

"I mean other than Rick Hartman," Clint said.

"I don't know who Ruth knew," he said. "If that's what you mean. She had that shop, I assume had a lot of customers."

"You didn't know her friends?"

"No," Kellog said, "we're not—weren't that close."

"How close were you?"

"Not at all, really," Kellog said.

"I heard you asked her to marry you."

"What?" Crockett said.

"That was a long time ago," Kellog said. "She said no, and that was it."

"And you took it, just like that?"

"What, you think I waited five years to kill her because she turned down my proposal?"

"No, I doubt that," Clint said.

"I thought I needed a wife back then, and she seemed suitable. Since then, I've decided I'm fine on my own."

Clint looked at Crockett, who was being very quiet.

"Did you know Ruth Bridges?" Clint asked.

"What, me? No, why would I know 'er? She ran a dress shop, right?" Crockett shook his head. "There'd be no reason for me to know 'er."

"Just thought I'd ask," Clint said. He looked at Kellog again. "What're you going to do with that Tobiano now that it's broke?"

"Probably sell it," the man said. "That's what I do with horses."

"Too bad," Clint said. "That's an unusual animal. The coloring, and all."

"You wanna trade for yours?" Kellog asked. "Straight up?"

"What? No!" Clint said. The idea of trading Eclipse for any horse was staggering.

"Just a thought," Kellog said. "I know it's a gelding and can't be bred, but if you ever decide to get rid of it, let me know."

"Don't hold your breath while you're waiting," Clint advised.

Kellog laughed and said, "Understood. Tim, why don't you show Mr. Adams out?"

"Sure thing, boss. This way, Mr. Adams."

Clint followed the foreman to the front door and out.

"Is there something you might want to tell me that you didn't mention in front of your boss?" Clint asked, as they walked down the front steps.

"Whataya mean?" Crockett asked.

"You seemed a little quiet when we were talking about Ruth Bridges," Clint said. "You sure you didn't know her?"

Crockett looked around, then said, "Let's get away from the house."

They walked together toward the barn, but not near the corral, where some of the cowpokes were still admiring Toby.

"All right," Crockett said, "I did know Ruth, but I don't want my boss getting' wind of it."

"Of what?"

"Well . . . I kinda asked her to marry me, too."

"And?"

"She said no."

"Did she say why not?"

"She didn't want to live on a ranch," he said. "Same thing she told Mr. Kellog. So if she didn't wanna live with the owner, she sure as hell didn't wanna live with the foreman."

"I see."

"Look," Crockett said, "she was a beautiful woman. "She had plenty of men in town after her."

"Can you name any?"

"No," he said, "but just talk to any single man between fifteen and fifty and they'll tell ya they wanted her.

"But she wanted Rick Hartman."

"Apparently."

"All right, Mr. Crockett," Clint said. "Thanks for talking to me."

"Well, thanks for breaking the Tobiano."

Clint mounted Eclipse.

47

"To tell you the truth," he said, "I don't think he's broke."

"What?"

"Without Eclipse around," Clint said, "I don't think anybody else is going to be able to ride him."

"Well, goddamn," Crockett said, as Clint rode off.

Chapter Twelve

When Clint got back to Labyrinth, he dropped Eclipse off at the livery stable. The rest of what he had to do he could do on foot. The names Lily had given him were all in town.

But he was also concerned with what the foreman, Tim Crockett had told him, that a lot of men in town were after Ruth Bridges. He wondered if Rick knew that.

Before talking to anyone else—including Rick—he decided to stop by Rick's Place for a beer, and a talk with Shiloh. Since the bartender had gone with Rick for his midnight meeting that never took place, he might know something.

***

The place was still not busy, even though it was afternoon. In the past, when Clint had stayed in Labyrinth for several days at a time, Rick's Place was always busy, except for early mornings.

"What's going on?" he asked Shiloh, leaning on the bar.

"How do you mean?"

"There's usually more customers here."

Shiloh stopped cleaning glasses and also leaned on the bar.

"It used to be that Rick's Place was pretty much the only place in town to have a good time. That's changed. Other places have opened."

"Saloons?"

"Saloons, gambling parlors . . . pleasure palaces."

"You mean whorehouses?"

"They call themselves pleasure palaces," Shiloh said. "They offer drinks, gambling, women, and I don't mean just saloon girls."

"Where are these places?"

"All over," Shiloh said, "but you haven't ridden through town, have you?"

"No, I've been busy."

"There's a whole new section in the south end, and a lot of places are there."

"You mean . . . there's a red light district, now? Like in Dodge City?"

Shiloh stood up straight.

"I never thought of it that way, but yeah, that. Where'd that term come from, anyway?"

"There used to be an establishment in Dodge called The Red Light Saloon. It was a haven for pickpockets and prostitutes, and pretty soon the term described the entire area. Then they started using it in Tombstone, as well."

"Yeah, well, I guess we got one here, now," Shiloh said. "Labyrinth's been growin' since you been away, Clint, and not in a good way."

"I'm starting to see that."

"How's the boss doin'?"

"You know Rick," Clint said. "He's bearing up. But I want to get him out of there."

"You wanna break him out?" Shiloh asked. "I'm with ya."

"No, I want to get him out legally," Clint said.

"How can I help?"

"What can you tell me about that night you went with him to meet someone at the stockyards?"

"They didn't show up."

"That's it?"

"What more is there?" Shiloh asked. "He told me to stay back and he went into the yard. Next thing I know, he's back and he says whoever it was didn't show up."

"Any reason not to believe him?" Clint asked.

"No," Shiloh said. "Why would he lie about that?"

"I don't know," Clint said. "I'll ask next time I talk to him."

"When's that gonna be?" Shiloh asked.

"Later today, but he did say he wants to keep this place open."

"I can do that," Shiloh said. "Tell 'im not to worry."

"I will."

As Clint started for the door, Shiloh called out, "Oh, and tell 'im I tried to see 'im, but the sheriff wouldn't let me."

Clint waved and left.

***

He stopped in at several of the businesses on the list Lily had given him. Most of the owners were men. One was a woman, who had nothing good to say about Ruth Bridges.

"She had so many of the men in town sniffing after her," Harriet Webb said. She owned something called a "milliner's shop." Clint had to look in the window to discover that meant hats. "Like dogs in heat," she added.

"So you didn't like her?"

"Not many women in town did," she said. "Not all the men sniffing after her were unmarried."

"Ah," Clint said, "and do you know if she . . . encouraged any of these married men?"

"She certainly didn't discourage them," the middle-aged shop owner said. "But if you're asking me if I know of any she actually cheated with, the answer is no."

"All right, then. Mrs. Webb," he said. "Thank you."

As he'd already been told, the men all spoke of her in glowing terms. They were obviously enamored of her.

"All I would've needed was a hint," one of them, an older man, said, "and I would've left my wife in a minute."

"But she never gave that hint?"

"The only one she gave anything to was Rick Hartman," the man said, "and it was more than just a hint."

Chapter Thirteen

"This is gettin' to be a habit," Sheriff Ritter said as Clint entered.

Clint took his gun out and handed it over.

"If you'd let him out, I wouldn't have to do this."

"That's up to Judge Wilkie."

Ritter took Clint into the cellblock and left him there.

"What now?" Rick asked. This time he just remained seated on the cot.

"I want to know if the picture I'm getting of Ruth Bridges is right."

"Why? What've you been hearing?"

Clint told Rick everything he'd been told so far, by Lily, Kellog, Crockett, and the other tradesmen he'd talked to, including the woman, Harriet Webb.

"This Webb woman sounds jealous," Rick said.

"How about what the others said?" Clint asked.

"It sounds about right," Rick replied. "She was beautiful and sought after."

"By married and single men."

"Yes," Rick said, "but from what she told me, she hadn't been with any married men."

"Did you believe her?"

"To tell you the truth, I didn't care," Rick said. "I've been with my share of married women. Haven't you?"

Too many, Clint thought. It had once been a rule of his not to sleep with married women, but of late that rule seemed to have fallen by the wayside occasionally.

"Never mind," he said.

"I'll tell you what I believe," Rick said. "She wasn't seeing anybody but me, and the men in town didn't like that."

"Then wouldn't it have been more likely for one of them to try to kill you, and not her?"

"Unless we're dealing with a coward," Rick pointed out. "Then it was easier for him to kill a woman and put the blame on me."

"How did he put the blame on you?"

"My story is," Rick said, "when she was killed, I was in the stockyards, waiting to meet somebody."

"So he got you out into the stockyards, which are still part of town, so he could kill her, and you'd have no alibi. What about Shiloh?"

"He didn't see me *in* the stockyards," Rick said. "I left him outside."

"He could've lied for you."

"I don't believe he thought of it, at the time."

"All right," Clint said, "let me get together with your lawyer and see what we can do."

"What do you think of him?"

"So far I think he's all right," Clint said, "but he and Judge Wilkie don't get along."

"That makes two of us."

"What does Wilkie have against you?"

"I kicked him out of my place the first time he ever came in."

"Why?"

"He got grabby with one of the girls," Rick said. "Now he crosses into the red light district to do his grabbing."

"I heard about the new south end of town," Clint said. "I'm going to have to go and have a look."

"Don't start doing your drinking and gambling over there," Rick said. "You'll get your pocket picked before you know it."

"So Labyrinth is turning into Dodge City?" Clint asked.

"Hardly," Rick said, "but it's trying."

"Do you think somebody from that side did this to you?" Clint asked.

"It would make sense," Rick said. "I still have the top place in town."

"So then this may have nothing to do with Ruth Bridges and her life," Clint said. "She may have just got caught up in a vendetta against you."

"It's starting to look that way, isn't it?" Rick asked, sadly. "Men loved her, and the women in town wouldn't have cut her throat."

"Then I have to look at this in a whole new light," Clint said. "Red light district here I come. Tell me, who's your biggest competitor, over there?"

"Nobody," Rick said, "but I'll tell you who thinks they are . . ."

***

Clint collected his gun from Sheriff Ritter, told the man nothing, and headed for Raymond Judd's office. When he got there, he entered and found the man seated at his desk.

"You've got something," Judd said, looking up at him. "I can tell."

"I may," Clint said, and started to explain. Judd listened without interrupting, which impressed Clint.

"So you're goin' to the red light district tonight?" Judd asked, when Clint was finished.

"I am."

"You mind some company?" Judd asked.

"Have you been there before?"

"A time or two," Judd admitted.

"Then by all means, come along."

Chapter Fourteen

Clint met Judd outside his office at seven o'clock, and they walked to the far end of town, then crossed into the red light district. There was no noticeable distinction between the streets. The difference was probably in the saloons, gambling houses and pleasure palaces.

"Do you know where the Princess Pleasure Palace is?" Clint asked.

"I think so. Why?"

"According to Rick, the man who owns it has it in for him," Clint answered. "His name's . . . August Dewey?"

"Auggie Dewey, yeah, I know him," Judd said. "Never thought he was such a bad guy, but then he's got nothin' against me. I did a job for him, once."

"What kind of job?" Clint asked.

"Just the paperwork for his business," Judd said.

"How long has the place been open?"

"All of these places over here have been open a matter of months."

"How does the mayor feel about his town having a red light district?"

"Are you kiddin'?" Judd asked. "It was his idea."

"Well, let's start there," Clint said.

"It's this way . . ."

***

The building was so new it still smelled of fresh wood. It was two-stories high, and every window was brightly lit.

Most whorehouses had locked doors that you had to knock on, and you wouldn't always be admitted, depending on who you were and what time it was. However, the Princess Pleasure Palace was wide open, allowing anybody to walk in.

Once inside, there was loud piano music, the sound of chips hitting the gaming tables, girls working the floor in suggestive varieties of dress and what could only be called *un*dress. The bar that was doing a damned good business. The décor was gaudy; portraits of nude women decorated the walls, bright crystal, and splashy colors filled every available space.

The place shrieked "pleasure."

"Rick was wrong," Clint said to Judd.

"What'd he say?"

"That this place was no competition for his," Clint answered.

"Oh yes," Judd said, "I think he's wrong, too."

They went to the bar, where Clint quickly had to brush off the attention of two pickpockets, and one whore.

The bartender brought them two beers at Clint's request, then frowned when Clint asked for August Dewey.

The barman was big, probably doubled as a bouncer, so he glared at Clint in a menacing fashion and asked, "Whatchoo want with Auggie?"

"Just to talk."

"About what?"

"Murder."

"Yeah?" the man asked. "Who got murdered?"

"I'd rather talk to him about it."

"You got a name, friend?"

"Clint Adams."

The bartender straightened up and the look on his face changed to one of concern.

"Oh, uh, just wait a second, Mr. Adams," he said. "I'll find 'im."

"Thank you."

As the bartender moved away, Judd asked, "Does your name always work magic?"

"Sometimes," Clint said, "it just gets me shot at."

They worked on their beers until the bartender came back.

"Who's he?" he asked, looking at Judd.

"My lawyer," Clint said, "And Mr. Dewey's lawyer."

"Oh, yeah," the man said. "I recognize ya. Okay, follow me."

He led them to a back room that was not an office. Rather, it looked like a private gaming room not in use, at the moment.

"Boss, this is Clint Adams," the bartender said.

Clint stared.

August Dewey was a woman, and a good looking one, at that. She was sitting at a large, round, green felt-topped poker table.

"Mr. Judd didn't tell you?" she asked Clint, with a wide smile.

"No," Clint said, "He didn't, and neither did your bartender."

The bartender backed out quickly.

"I wanted it to be a surprise," Judd said.

And, as a matter of fact, Clint thought, Rick Hartman hadn't told him, either. It was nice to see that time behind bars hadn't affected his sense of humor.

"Mr. Adams," August Dewey said, "why don't you have a seat and tell me what's on your mind?"

Chapter Fifteen

"Rick Hartman," Clint said.

"What about him?" she asked. "I heard he's in jail for murder."

"Yes, for killing a woman named Ruth Bridges."

"I knew Ruth," August said. "I bought some dresses from her. She was a lovely lady." This coming from a woman who, herself, was a lovely redhead in her forties, who still had smooth, freckled shoulders and breasts, shown off well by a green gown.

"Yes, she was."

"And you're friends with Mr. Hartman," she said.

"I am."

She looked at Judd.

"And you're his lawyer?"

"Yes."

"A little different from the work you did for me, isn't it?" she asked.

"I was appointed by the judge."

"Judge Wilkie," she said. "I see."

"You know him?"

She smiled.

"The Judge is a good customer."

"Well, he's trying to railroad Rick," Clint said. "I intend to stop him."

"And you want my help?"

"Rick tells me you're his biggest competition."

She laughed.

"I'm surprised he thought any of us on this side of the district were competition for him."

"Well, what he said was, if anyone was competition, it was you."

"That I can believe," she said. "So how do you think I can help you?"

"I've decided that whoever killed Ruth Bridges was after Rick, not her."

"You mean they wanted him to go down for murderin' her," she said.

"Yes."

"And you think that was me?"

"Was it?"

"No."

"Then I don't think it was."

"You'll take my word for that?"

"Sure, why not?"

"I could be lying."

"Have you been known to lie?" he asked.

"Yes," she said, "with good reason."

"But not now."

"I have no reason to lie to you, Mr. Adams."

"Then I guess you better call me Clint."

"And you can call me Auggie," she said.

"I think," Ray Judd said, "I'll go to the bar and get a drink." He waved with his empty beer mug.

"I'll meet you out there, Ray," Clint said.

"Miss Dewey," Judd said, and left.

"I can have a drink brought in for you and me if you like, Clint," Auggie said.

"I don't think I'll be here that long," he said. "Does Judge Wilkie drink here, or does he go upstairs with the girls? I assume the rooms are upstairs?"

"They are, and he does," Auggie said.

"So, as one of your customers, he'd be happy to see Rick's Place close."

"I guess so," she said. "But I wouldn't."

"Why not?"

"There's room for all of us," she said. "Labyrinth is growing, and Rick's Place is an institution, hereabouts. Don't you think?

"Oh, I do," he said.

"So while I can't speak for the Judge, or for any of the other saloon owners," she said, "I don't want to see Rick's Place close down."

"Do you know anybody who does?" he asked. "Specifically?"

"Other than the Judge, you mean?" She nodded. "There may be one or two gentlemen on this side of the district who would, yes."

"Would any of them be on this list?" he asked, showing her the names Lily gave him.

She read and returned it.

"No," she said, "the people on that list are decent folks, much like Ruth was. The men who want him to go out of business are irredeemable louts, I'm afraid."

"And would you have a few names?"

"One or two," she said.

He returned the list to her and gave her the stub of a pencil he had in his pocket, and she added the names.

"Now I'm curious," he said. "Why would you supply me with these names?"

"Because," she said, "those are men whose establishments I wouldn't mind seeing close down."

"And would you lie to me to make that happen?"

She smiled at him and said, "No?"

Chapter Sixteen

When Clint stood up to leave Auggie said, "Come back some time, as a customer."

"I'll come back for a drink," he said, "but I don't pay for pleasure."

"I don't suppose you ever need to," she said. "Then just come back for a visit."

"I will, Auggie," he said. "Thanks for seeing me."

"Why wouldn't I want to see the Gunsmith?" she asked. She stood up. "I'll walk you out."

She put her arm through his and accompanied him out to the bar. People greeted her along the way, looked at the two of them curiously.

They stopped at the bar where Ray Judd was drinking another beer.

"One for the road?" Auggie asked Clint.

"I don't think so, Auggie," Clint said. "I think I'll be having a few more along the way."

She slapped a pickpocket's hand away from his side and said, "Then I'll see you again, some time. Just ask for me."

"I will. Thanks."

Ray Judd finished his beer, nodded to Auggie, and walked out with Clint.

"Where to now?" Judd asked.

They had walked away from the Princess Pleasure Palace and down the street before Clint stopped.

"Auggie gave me two names," he said. "Dean Macklin runs a place called The Phoenix Palace, and Elvis Bohannon runs the Salvation Saloon. Have you ever heard such a name?"

"Salvation—I know where that one is."

"Then let's go," Clint said. "If nothing else, I've got to find out what's behind that name."

***

Judd showed Clint the way to the Salvation Saloon. There was piano music coming from inside as they entered, but rather than saloon music, it sounded like a church hymn. Over the bar, where there was usually a painting of a horse, or a naked nymph, was a crucifix.

"I don't believe this," Clint said.

The man behind the bar wore a shirt, suspenders, and a clerical collar. His face had deep lines which had apparently not come from age, since he didn't seem to be forty, yet.

"What the hell—" Clint said.

"You'll see," Judd said.

They approached the bar and the bartender acknowl-
edged them with a nod.

"Gents."

"Two beers, please," Clint said.

"Comin' up."

The bartender, in the clerical collar, drew two beers
and set them down.

"I'm looking for a man named Elvis Bohannon."

"That'd be me," the man said, "but I go by Father Elvis."

"Father . . . you're a priest."

"I am," the man said. "Properly ordained."

"And this is your church?"

"It is." The man smiled. "I can see you're confused."

"Slightly, Father."

"What do most churches have in common, my
friend?" Father Elvis asked.

"Um . . . sinners?"

"They're poor," the priest said. "My church is not,
and yes, that is because I serve many sinners. It says
Salvation Saloon outside, but this is actually the Salvation
Church."

"I see."

"So what is it I can do for you, my son?" Father Elvis
asked, leaning on the bar.

"I'm here on behalf of Rick Hartman."

"Ah, I understand poor Rick is having some difficulties."

"If you can call being arrested for murder 'difficulties,' then yes."

"And you're his friend."

"I'm his friend, and Mr. Judd, here, is his lawyer."

"Ah, I thought you looked familiar, Mr. Judd. Been in here before?"

"Once or twice."

"Seeking salvation?"

"Seeking beer," Judd said.

Father Elvis looked at Clint.

"In your attempt to clear your friend you're looking for others to blame the murder on, I suppose."

"Not blame," Clint said. "I'm looking for whoever actually killed Ruth Bridges."

"Well, sadly, I didn't know the woman," Father Elvis said. "Can I ask who gave you my name?"

"I'd rather not say," Clint replied.

"That's all right," Father Elvis said, "I believe I know. How is Miss Dewey, anyway?"

Clint didn't answer.

"Well," Father Elvis said, standing straight up, "let me tell you, I didn't know the woman and had no reason to want her dead."

"What about putting Rick's Place out of business?"

"Why would I want to do that?" Father Elvis asked. "His place is my biggest supplier of sinners."

Clint frowned. The priest had a point.

***

"That was odd," Clint said, standing in front of the Salvation Saloon. "One of the oddest places I've ever been and one of the oddest men. After him and Auggie, you got any more surprises for me over here?"

"Nope, that was it," Judd said. "Thought I'd have a laugh or two."

"I'll be sure to tell Rick Hartman that you're looking for laughs while we're trying to get him out of jail."

"I'm sure he'll appreciate it," Judd said.

Clint stared at Judd for a long moment, then nodded his head.

"Yeah, I guess he would."

Chapter Seventeen

Judd walked Clint over to the Phoenix Palace, which presented a much more familiar picture than the Salvation Saloon had.

They entered the Phoenix and found it a lively place, which would be expected of red light district establishments.

"Do you know Macklin?" Clint asked.

"Never met him," Judd said.

"Are you sure?"

"I told you," Judd replied. "No more surprises."

"Just checking . . ." Clint said.

They went to the bar and ordered two beers. They had to use their elbows to create spaces, which was received with laughter from other men at the bar.

"This is a cheerful place," Clint commented.

"That's the best kind," Judd said. "I hate places filled with nasty drunks."

Clint called the bartender back. He was a happy fella, with a big smile on his young face.

"Somethin' else?" he asked.

"Is Dean Macklin around?"

"Mr. Macklin likes to stay on the floor during business hours," the bartender said. "He's probably at one of the poker tables." The man pointed.

"What am I looking for?" Clint asked.

"A well-dressed fella who smells of lilac water," the bartender said, wrinkling his nose. "He's kinda old . . . about your age."

"Thanks," Clint said.

"I'll just wait here and work on my beer," Judd said.

"I won't be long," Clint promised.

Clint walked in the direction the bartender had pointed, taking his beer with him. Even in the smoky atmosphere of the saloon, he smelled the lilac water before he even reached the table. When he got there, he saw five men holding their cards close to their chests, only one of which was well-dressed and reeking of lilac. Clint waited for the hand to be over, so his interruption wouldn't affect the outcome. Dean Macklin won the hand with three queens.

"Dean Macklin?" Clint said, while the man raked in his chips.

"That's me," Macklin said, looking up. "Who're you?"

"My name's Clint Adams."

Macklin sat back in his chair with a look of surprise on his face.

"Really?"

"Yes, really. Can we talk?"

"About what?" Macklin asked.

"Murder."

Macklin looked even more surprised.

"Deal me out, gents," Macklin said, "but watch my chips."

He stood up, revealing himself to be several inches shorter than Clint.

"You trust them with your chips?" Clint asked.

"Oh, I know all those boys," Macklin said. "They're good fellas. None of them would steal from me. Let's go over here to my private table."

He led the way to an empty table, and as soon as they sat, a saloon girl appeared.

"Can I get you and your guest something, Mr. Macklin?" she asked.

Dean Macklin looked at Clint, who said, "I'm good with this."

"Just one beer, Lori, thanks," Macklin said.

"Yessir."

She flounced off.

"Well, Mr. Adams," Macklin said, "to what do I owe the pleasure of a visit from the Gunsmith?"

Chapter Eighteen

"And what was that about murder?" Macklin asked.

"Ruth Bridges."

"Ah, the lovely Miss Bridges," Macklin said. "Rick Hartman's in jail for that murder, isn't he?"

"He didn't do it."

"Who says?" Macklin asked.

"He does," Clint answered, "and so do I."

"Well, I'd expect him to deny it," Macklin said, "but why do you?"

"Because I know Rick," Clint said.

"Are you saying he isn't capable of murder?" Macklin asked. "Because I think we all are, given the right circumstances."

"I do too," Clint said, "but cutting a woman's throat is not the right circumstance."

"I see," Macklin said. "And what is it you want from me?"

"I was just wondering if you knew Ruth Bridges," Clint replied. "From what you just said, I assume you did."

"I did know her, yes," Macklin said. "So?"

"So," Clint said, "I was wondering if you knew of anyone else who might have wanted her dead."

"Not a one."

"Then Macklin, you know somebody who'd want Rick Hartman to go to jail for murder? Thereby causing his place to close?"

"Oh, now I get it," Macklin said. "You think I want Rick's Place to close up. Why would I want that?"

"Competition," Clint said.

"And I'd want that bad enough to kill for it?" Macklin said. "Look at this place." He spread his arms, sending a lilac aroma Clint's way. "Do I really look like I need more business?"

The man had a good point. There were no empty tables, and no room at the bar.

"But," Clint said, "everybody needs business."

"I'm pretty happy with the way my place is going, Adams," Macklin said. "You tell your friend Hartman I had nothing to do with Ruth's death. You and him, you're gonna have to look somewhere else for your killer."

"Oh, I'll tell him," Clint said, "but he didn't give me your name."

"I'm sure my name came to you from any number of other sources," Macklin said. "Auggie Dewey, Father Elvis, Stan Baker. Whoever gave it to you, you can cross me off your list."

Clint made a mental note of the name "Stan Baker" and, as the girl came back with Macklin's beer, Clint stood and said, "Sorry to interrupt your game."

"No problem," Macklin said, accepting the beer from the girl, "I'll just go back and pick up where I left off."

"Good luck."

"I don't need luck," Macklin said. "I make my own."

Clint walked back to the bar and joined Judd there.

"Anything?" Judd asked.

"Says he had nothing to do with it."

"And you believed him?"

"I did."

"So what now?"

"I've had too much beer and not enough to eat," Clint said. "Is there a place in this district?"

"A few," Judd said. "I know of one that's not bad."

"Let's go, then."

Judd nodded, put down his empty mug, and led the way out.

***

Judd took Clint to a small, no-name café he would never have found on his own. And if he had, he wouldn't have gone inside.

"Don't worry," Judd said. "It's better than it looks."

"How do you know?"

"The owner's a client of mine," Judd said. "I helped him get started."

"And you've eaten here?"

"A time or two," Judd said. "Stick with the beef stew. The owner's Irish."

They went inside, took a table in the back of the near empty café.

"Mr. Judd," a red-haired man said, coming over.

"Hello, Mickey," Judd said. "This is my friend, Clint Adams. Clint, Mickey O'Neil."

"Mr. O'Neil," Clint said.

"Just call me Mickey, sir."

"All right, Mickey. My friend here tells me to order the beef stew."

"Mulligan Stew," Mickey said, proudly. "And you, Mr. Judd?"

"The stew, Mickey."

"Comin' up."

"And two beers," Judd added.

Mickey, bandy-legged and middle-aged, nodded and hurried to the kitchen.

"What do we do after we eat, Clint?" Judd asked.

"We ask more questions, Mr. Judd," Clint said. "We ask more questions."

Chapter Nineteen

Judd took Clint to two more saloons and another pleasure palace, waited while he talked with the owners. When he was done it was getting dark, and they decided to head back to the center of town and Rick's Place.

"Tell me," Judd said, as they walked, "do you think you can always tell when somebody is lying?"

"No, not necessarily."

"But you believed the people you spoke to today?"

"Unfortunately, I did," Clint said. "None of them had time to think. They didn't know I was coming."

"You don't think they had a story ready for the sheriff?" Judd asked.

"Probably not."

"So where does that leave us?"

"Back where we started," Clint said. "Believing Rick is innocent."

Judd didn't react to that.

"I never asked you," Clint said. "Do *you* believe he's innocent?"

"It doesn't matter what I think," Judd said. "I'm supposed to defend him."

"Yes, but wouldn't it be easier for you to defend him if you believed he didn't do it?"

"I can't really discuss that," Judd said. "Look, I've got to go to my office for a bit, and then I'm going to turn in. Let me know what you want to do tomorrow. I'll be in my office."

"Yes, all right," Clint said. "Good-night, then."

As Judd broke away and headed for his office, Clint wondered if Rick was being defended by the right man? Of course, Judge Wilkie assigned Judd for his own reasons, one of which might've been he didn't like either man and felt they wouldn't get along.

If Clint could get Rick out of jail, one of the first things his friend might have to do was find a lawyer he trusted.

Clint continued toward Rick's Place.

***

Shiloh saw Clint as he entered and had a beer up on the bar by the time he got there.

"Hard day?" the bartender asked.

"Lots of talking," Clint said, "not much accomplished."

"So you're not gettin' the boss out?"

"Not yet." Clint sipped his beer. "It's been a long day. I'm going to turn in."

"I'm sure the boss wouldn't mind if you slept upstairs in his room."

"No, that's all right," Clint said. "I already have a hotel room."

"Well, lemme know if there's anythin' I can do," Shiloh said.

"I will," Clint said. "I told Rick you tried to get in to see him. He appreciates it."

"Thanks, Clint."

Clint took one more sip, then put the beer mug down and said, "'night."

Clint left Rick's Place and headed for his hotel.

***

The three men met in the darkened back room.

"Clint Adams is in town," said Third.

"We know that," First said. "That's why we're meeting here again."

"So whataya wanna do about it?" Second asked.

"I don't know," First said. "It depends on how much damage we think he can do."

"He's the goddamned Gunsmith," Second said.

"None of us are going to go up against him with a gun, are we?" First asked.

"I sure ain't," Second said.

"How far has he got so far?" Third asked.

"Not far," First said.

"So what do we do?" Second asked.

"We keep an eye on him," First said, "watch his progress. If he starts to get close, then we'll have to do something."

"Like what?" Third asked.

"We have time to think about that," First said.

"So what do we do in the meantime?" Second asked.

"We just keep doing what we've been doing," First said. "This town's going to grow, and it's going to be ours."

"That's the plan," Second said. "But we didn't figure on the Gunsmith."

"I did," First said.

"What?" Third asked.

"When we picked Rick Hartman, I knew there was a possibility Clint Adams would get involved."

"So then you have a plan," Second said.

"I do have a plan," First said, then added, "sort of."

"Whataya mean, sort of," Second said.

"I'm still working on it," First said. "Let's get the hell out of here so I can work out the particulars."

Second and Third looked at each other, then followed First out.

Chapter Twenty

Clint woke the next morning, needing breakfast and a haircut. Breakfast was easy to get in the hotel dining room. He wanted the haircut just to see if Melanie Jones was still in town.

He had met the lady barber two visits back, had been pleased to find her still there the last time he was in town. Now if he found her again, at least he'd have somebody in Labyrinth he could halfway trust. Their relationship had progressed to that point. But with the changes taking place in town, there was the possibility she had left. After all, she liked the town because it was what she called "quaint." But it sure as hell wasn't that anymore, not when it had a red light district.

He left the hotel and walked to the barber shop. He was happy to see, before he even reached it, Melanie Jones through the front window. She must have had a customer already that morning, as she was sweeping her floor. He knew she did that after every cut, to get ready for the next.

As he opened the door and entered, she looked up from her sweeping and smiled when she saw him. Her long dark hair was even longer, hanging past her shoulders and, as usual, she was wearing jeans and a man's shirt.

"Well, look what the cat dragged in," she said.

"Hey, Mel."

She dropped the broom and leaped into his arms. He kissed her soundly and then hugged her tightly.

"It's so good to see you, Clint," she said, holding him at arm's length. "Have you seen what's happened to this town?"

"I have," he said. "I got here yesterday."

She slapped his shoulder and stepped back.

"You've been here a full day and just came to see me now?" she demanded.

"I had to go and see Rick first."

"Oh God!" she said, putting her hands over her mouth. "I heard about that. How terrible. So that's why you're here, to help him?"

"I'm here to try," he said. "I talked to some people yesterday, and have to continue today, but I wanted to stop and see you."

"Can I help?"

"I don't know," he said. "Did you know Ruth Bridges?"

"I met her," Mel said. "I bought something in her shop once, but I can't say I knew her."

"Then you wouldn't have any idea who killed her."

"None," she said. "Are you sure it wasn't Mr. Hartman?"

"Positive," Clint said. "I'm thinking it was somebody who wanted Rick to take the blame."

"But why?"

"To get him put away and force his saloon to go out of business."

"Ah, so his competition."

"Right."

"Well, there are a lot of those in town, now, especially in the red light district."

"I know," Clint said. "I was there yesterday. And I'll be going back today."

"So . . . will we have any time to be together?" she asked him.

"How about supper tonight?" Clint said. "I'll come back here at five o'clock to get you."

"Perfect," she said. "I'll look forward to it."

He kissed her again and said, "Sorry I've got to go."

"I understand," she said. "Go."

He went to the door, then looked back.

"I'm glad you're here," she said.

"So am I."

He went out.

***

When he entered the lawyer's office, he bypassed the outer office and went right to the main one. Judd was seated behind his desk.

"Good-morning," Judd said. "Have breakfast?"

"Yes, at my hotel."

"Good, I already ate, too," Judd said. "So we can get started."

"What's on your mind?"

"I was going to have another talk with Judge Wilkie today," Judd said. "I'll try one more plea to get Rick out of jail on bail."

"That sounds good," Clint said. "And I'll find some more people to talk to."

"You won't find anybody in the red light district," Judd told him. "Not this early."

"Not in the saloons," Clint said, "but maybe the pleasure palaces will be open."

"What do you think you'll find out there?"

"I don't know," Clint said. "Maybe I'll just go and talk to August Dewey again. Maybe she knows something she's not aware is important."

Chapter Twenty-One

Clint approached the Princess Pleasure Palace, which presented a very quiet picture that early. This time the door was closed, and he had to knock. The girl who answered was small, dark-haired, covered in a sheer but voluminous nightgown through which he could see dark pointed nipples on small breasts.

"We ain't open, handsome," she said, with her hand on her hip. "Come back later and ask for me, I'm Lisa."

"Thanks, Lisa, but right now I'm looking for Auggie."

She dropped her hand from her hip, and then the inviting look on her face, went from pretty to sulky.

"And who're you?" she asked.

"Clint Adams."

"Wait, I'll see if Auggie's awake."

She closed the door in his face rather emphatically, making him wonder if she was even going to come back. But she did . . .

"Auggie says she's been expectin' you," Lisa said. "Follow me."

She led the way down the hall, and he followed. They got to a closed door, at which time Lisa knocked, said, "Go ahead in," and walked away.

Clint entered.

Auggie was sitting at a table with what looked like a full breakfast in front of her. She was wearing a silk robe over a nightgown, with an impressive display of cleavage showing. "Mr. Adams," she said. "Welcome. Breakfast?"

"I'll have some coffee, thanks," he said.

"Please, have a seat."

He sat across from her as she poured him a cup of coffee.

"There's plenty of bacon here," she said. "I love bacon. Have some."

"Maybe just one slice," he said, grabbing a long one. "Lisa said you were expecting me."

"I was," she said. "I knew you'd want to talk with me again after you saw Father Elvis and the others."

"Father Elvis," Clint said. "That was almost as odd as finding out that August Dewey is a woman."

"I hope you're not disappointed," she said.

"Oh, not at all," he said, then added, "I mean, at least, not in you."

"Thank you."

He took a bite of the crisp bacon.

"Did you talk with Dean Macklin?" she asked.

"I did."

"What did you think of him?"

"I thought he was being honest with me."

"Dean has that effect on people."

"Is he always honest?" Clint asked.

She smiled.

"As long as you're not a woman," she said, chewing on some bacon. It seemed to be all she was having for breakfast, along with the coffee.

"Would you like something else?" she asked. "I can get you some biscuits, or eggs."

"No," he said, "I had my breakfast." He snagged another slice of bacon. "This is just really good bacon."

"I have my cook make it with maple syrup," she said.

"That's the flavor," Clint said. "I'll have to remember that."

"So I'm assuming you didn't find out very much last night that was helpful," Auggie said.

"You'd be right," Clint said. "But I got the feeling everybody, not just Macklin, was telling me the truth."

"Well, either that's the case," she said, "or you're very easy to fool. Are you?"

"Not usually," he said.

"How's Mr. Hartman doing?" she asked.

"Chafing to get out," Clint said.

"Why don't you just break him out, then?" she asked. "Isn't that what you men do?"

"I don't know what men you're talking about," Clint said, "but he'd still be wanted if I did that. No, I've got to get him out legally."

"I was just trying to be funny, Mr. Adams," she told him. "No offense meant."

"None taken."

"Well," Clint said, "since you were expecting me to come back, do you have any other information to share with me?"

"If I do," Auggie said, "I might want something in return."

"Like what?"

"I have a customer I don't like," she said. "I'd like him to stop coming here to be with my girls."

"Why's that?"

"He abuses them."

"Have him arrested," Clint suggested.

"I can't."

"Why not?"

"Because," she said, "it's Judge Wilkie."

"Ah . . . what do you expect me to do about it?"

"He'll be here tonight," she said. "Do with that whatever you will. Maybe it'll be useful to you."

"You know," Clint said, grabbing another piece of bacon, "it might, at that."

Chapter Twenty-Two

When the bacon was gone, Auggie stood up.

"Let's go to my sitting room."

"Lead the way."

Instead of leaving by the door he came in, she took him to another door, which led to a sitting room decorated in red and green. There was a large, plush divan, matching chairs, and another piece of furniture he recognized.

"That's a chaise lounge," he said.

"How do you know that?" she asked. "It's French."

"I've seen them before, in Chicago, Boston, and once in Denver. Usually, in the homes of rich people."

"I imported that one from Chicago," she told him.

"Impressive," he said, running his hand over it. It was soft, cushioned, and covered with green velvet.

"Don't get the idea I'm rich," she said. "I just saw it in a catalog and wanted it." She pointed to some dressing screens across the floor. "You mind if I get dressed?"

"No, not at all," he said. "Go ahead. You mind if I sit on your lounge?"

"Be my guest."

He went to the lounge, and she went around behind the screen.

***

"Breakfast," Sheriff Ritter said. He unlocked the cell door and handed Rick a tray.

"Thanks," Rick said.

He took the tray to his cot, sat and uncovered it. It was ham-and-eggs and coffee, as it had been every day since he'd been locked up. Luckily, he liked ham-and-eggs and coffee.

"Your buddy Adams is out there askin' a lot of people questions," Ritter said. "He seems determined to get you out of here."

"Yeah, he's stubborn that way."

"Whatayou think the chances are he'll decide to just break you out?" Ritter asked.

"None," Rick said. "He wants to get me out legally, which is the way I want to get out."

"What if you can't?"

"I better," Rick said, "since I didn't kill Ruth Bridges. I'm an innocent man, Sheriff."

"Well," Ritter said, "if you are, I hope he can prove it."

As the sheriff left him to eat his breakfast, Rick muttered, "So do I."

***

Ray Judd was allowed to see Judge Wilkie for ten minutes, and this time the Judge meant ten minutes.

"Make your plea, Mr. Judd," Wilkie said, sitting back in his chair, prepared to reject it. "And if you're going to ask me to assign another attorney, forget it. It would take too long to get someone else here."

"I wasn't going to ask that, Your Honor," Judd said.

"Then go ahead."

"Rick Hartman has strong ties to the community, sir," Judd said. "He's not going anywhere."

"If I let him out, and he's guilty, he'll run," the Judge said.

"Judge, he's not guilty—"

Wilkie put his hand up to stop the lawyer, "I'm not just going to take your word for that, Mr. Judd," he said.

"I didn't think you would, sir."

"Then what are you doing here?" Wilkie asked. "Do you have some guarantee that your client won't run?"

"Just my—"

"Other than your word."

"No, sir."

Wilkie looked at the clock.

"Then you've had seven minutes, and I think that's quite enough," Wilkie said. "Have a good day."

"Yes sir," Judd said. "Thank you, sir."

Judd stood up and left the judge's chambers.

***

The chaise lounge was extremely comfortable.

"You got your money's worth for this," Clint said to Auggie, who was still behind her screens.

"Did I?"

"I think I could probably sleep on this thing."

"Oh, I've fallen asleep on it a time or two," she told him. "Believe me."

He did. He put his head back, fought the urge to close his eyes.

"Of course," she said, "it's good for other things, too."

"Really?" he asked. "Like what?"

She stepped out from behind the screen, completely naked.

"What do you think?"

Chapter Twenty-Three

Clint couldn't say what he was thinking, because he was stunned into silence. She was a healthy woman in her forties, with curves in abundance. The hair between her majestic thighs was as red as the hair on her head, and her full, pear-shaped breasts were covered with freckles.

"I told you I expected you to come back," she said. "I saw the way you looked at me."

"Auggie—"

"And if you weren't looking at me that way then, you sure as hell are now," she added.

"Can't much help it, can I?" he asked. "You fill a room with everything a man could want." His eyes took in acres of pale flesh, while his nose breathed in the scent of her from across the room.

"You stay right there," she told him, as he started to get up. "I'll come to you."

She walked slowly across the room towards him as he watched, mesmerized.

"Goddamn, woman . . ." he breathed.

As she approached, he could feel the heat coming off her body.

"I'm thinking you need to relax," she said, putting her hands on him.

"I'm anything but relaxed, right now," he told her.

She pressed her hands to the front of his trousers and said, "I can feel that. But I want to see it."

"I thought the boss in these places didn't entertain," he said.

"You're a special case," she said.

"Remember," he said, as she undid his trousers, "I told you I don't pay for my pleasure."

"I don't, either," she said, "so that makes us even."

Before attempting to remove his trousers, she pulled off his boots. After he removed his gunbelt and set it within easy reach, she slid his pants off. When she eased his underwear off, his hard cock sprang into view, to her delight. Meanwhile, he was able to actually watch her russet nipples become distended.

"Oh my," she said, sliding both her hands around his cock. She got down to her knees so she could give it all the attention she thought it deserved. She leaned in, rubbed it over her cheeks, then ran her tongue over it, which also went a long way toward making it difficult for him to relax.

When she took him into her mouth completely, he caught his breath. He wanted nothing more than to fill his hands with her abundant flesh, but he wasn't quite ready to pull himself from her mouth, yet, and he let her suck him for a while. Finally, he couldn't take it anymore.

"Okay," he said, reaching for her, "it's time to see if your chaise longue can take both of us."

She laughed and crawled up on top of him.

"I was wondering how long you could take it," she said.

"I hope you were impressed."

"I was."

She sat on him, trapping his hard cock between them, and unbuttoned his shirt. When she had removed it and tossed it away, she leaned over and began to kiss his chest. At the same time, she lifted her hips and he slid into her hot, wet pussy, with a groan from both of them.

She kissed his mouth, then, while undulating her hips in a circle, rather than ride him up and down. He reached for her breasts and they filled his hands to overflowing. Then she switched her movements and started to glide up and down on his hard cock. He put his hands on her generous hips and tried to match her rhythm. At the same time, he became aware of the chaise lounge groaning beneath them, but it continued to hold their weight.

She leaned forward so he could take her nipples into his mouth while she rode him, and gasped when he bit her.

"Harder," she implored him. "Bite me harder."

"Auggie—"

"Come on!" she said, bouncing up and down even harder.

Her breasts began to bounce about in front of him, so it was difficult to keep them in his mouth. But when he managed to capture one, he bit it hard and she squealed.

Then she grabbed his head in both hands and crushed his face to her breasts as waves of pleasure went crashing through her . . . and then he blew!

***

This time Auggie went behind her screens to get dressed. When she came out wearing a red gown, Clint was strapping his gun back on.

"That was nice," she said. "It's been a while for me."

"Why's that?" Clint asked. "I'm sure there are plenty of men in this town who'd want what I just got."

"Maybe there are," she said, "but they don't deserve it."

"What about Judge Wilkie?"

"Wilkie?" She laughed. "He doesn't want me. He only wants young girls. The kind who bruise easily."

"Why don't I come back tonight and catch him at it," Clint said. "Maybe we can both get something we want."

"Agreed," she said. "I'll see you then.

Chapter Twenty-Four

Later that night Judge Wilkie came out of his chambers. His clerk looked up at him.

"Heading home, Judge?" he asked.

"Not right away, Vincent," Wilkie said. "I'll see you in the morning."

"Yes, sir."

Wilkie left the building and walked through the darkening streets to the Princess Pleasure Palace.

"Good-evening, Judge," Lisa said, hoping the man wouldn't choose her tonight.

"Lisa," he said.

"I'll tell Auggie you're here."

"You do that."

She went off down the hall, came back with Auggie behind her.

"Jeremiah," she said.

"Good-evening, Auggie," Wilkie said. "You're looking lovely, as usual."

"Thank you. What's your pleasure tonight?" she asked.

"Blonde, I think," Wilkie said. "Jill, or Kate?"

"I think Jill is available," Auggie said. "I'll send her to you. Why don't you go up to your usual room?"

"Very well," Wilkie said.

He went up the stairs while Auggie went into the sitting room.

"He's upstairs," she said to Clint. "I'm supposed to send Jill."

Clint looked around, and a tall blonde put her hand up timidly.

"That'd be me," she said.

She was tall, slender and pretty.

"Have you been with Wilkie before?" he asked.

"Yes," she said.

"What does he do?"

"He'll hurt me," she said, "Leave bruises."

"Right away?"

"He'll want sex first," she said.

"I hate to ask—"

"That's her job," Auggie said, cutting him off.

"What happens after the sex?" he asked Jill.

"That's when the pain starts," Jill told him.

"Does he hit you?"

"Yes," she said, "and he . . . squeezes."

"Does he ever use a knife?" Clint asked. "Or anything with a blade?"

"No, he never has."

That would've been too easy.

"All right, Jill," Auggie said. "Up you go, then."

"Yes, Ma'am."

"I'll be up shortly," Clint promised.

"Not too soon," Auggie said. "Remember, he causes pain after the sex."

"Yes."

Jill nodded, and went up the stairs.

***

Wilkie was sitting on the bed with his back to the bedpost when Jill opened the door and entered.

"There's my lovely lady," Wilkie said.

"Hello, Judge."

She closed the door and pressed her back to it.

"Let me watch you undress."

"Yes, sir."

She peeled off her gown, revealing herself to be naked beneath. Her skin was pale, her breasts small with pink nipples. The hair at the apex of her thighs was fairer still than the hair on her head.

"Bring those long, lovely legs over here, my dear," Wilkie said.

"Yes, Judge."

She walked across the room to him . . .

***

"How long does he usually take?" Clint asked.

"Let's find out," Auggie said. "Lisa!"

The little brunette came walking over.

"You've been with Judge Wilkie a few times," Auggie began.

"Yes, Ma'am."

"Mr. Adams wants to know how long the Judge usually takes to finish."

"With me," Lisa said, "he's usually quick. With Jill, it'll be a little longer."

"Why's that?" Clint asked.

Lisa looked at him.

"She's not as good as I am," she said, and winked.

"When should I go up," he asked, "so that he doesn't hurt her too much?"

"You want him to hurt her a bit," Auggie said. "A bruise or two would be helpful."

Clint looked at Lisa.

"How long?"

"I'd say fifteen minutes or so, Mr. Adams."

Chapter Twenty-Five

Lisa had told Clint to wait fifteen minutes, but in twelve he started up the stairs. Auggie told him which room they were in.

He stopped at the door, pressed his ear to it, and when he heard a woman cry out in pain, he burst in. Jill was on the floor, naked, with Wilkie standing over her, also naked. He had hold of her wrist with one hand, and the other hand was raised, poised to strike her again.

"Let her go, Judge," Clint said. "We have some business to discuss."

"What?"

Clint put his hand on his gun.

"Let . . . her . . . go!"

"You have no right—"

"I heard a cry for help," Clint said. "I came in, saw someone beating her, and before I recognized you, I shot you dead to save her." He looked at the girl. "What do you think, Jill?"

"I'd swear to it," she said, harshly.

Wilkie released her wrist as if it had burned his hand.

"Get out of here, Jill," Clint said.

She grabbed her chemise, said, "Gladly," and ran for the door.

"You're overstepping your bounds, Adams," Wilkie said. He was so thin his ribs showed and, at the moment, his penis had shrunk and was hidden by the bush between his legs.

"Why don't you have a seat, Judge."

"I'd like my trousers," Wilkie said, pointing to the chair across the room.

"Not just yet."

Wilkie frowned, then sat and crossed his legs to hide his crotch.

"What's this about, Adams?" he asked.

"Oh, I think you know," Clint said. "It's come to my attention that you like to hurt women."

"Is that what's come to your attention?"

"I'm wondering how many other people in town know about it?"

"And you're going to tell them."

"I might."

"Unless I free Rick Hartman," Wilkie said. "Drop all charges."

"I don't think you can do that, Judge," Clint said, "but you can let him out on bail."

"This is blackmail," Wilkie said. "You're breaking the law."

"And you're not?" Clint asked. "Beating an innocent girl."

"They get paid," Wilkie said.

"For sex," Clint said, "not to get beat up."

"They're whores!" Wilkie shouted.

"Same answer," Clint said.

Wilkie frowned again. Clint noticed the man's body was now dappled with gooseflesh, either from being cold, or embarrassed.

"How about it, Judge?"

"You don't have any witnesses."

"I can bring a few more up, if you like," Clint offered. "But I think Jill's testimony would be enough."

"No," Wilkie said, "no more."

"And if anything happens to Jill . . ."

"I understand," Judge Wilkie said. "How did you get Auggie to go along with this?"

"Auggie has no idea," Clint lied.

"I'd be able to think better with my pants on," Wilkie said.

"What's there to think about, Judge?"

"How much bail to set for your friend," Wilkie said.

"In that case," Clint said, "put on your pants."

***

When Clint and Judge Wilkie came down the stairs none of the girls were in evidence.

"There," Clint said, waving his hand, "A clear path to the door."

Wilkie, now clad in his black suit and hat, glared at Clint and said, "This is not over."

"It is for now, Judge," Clint said. "Ray Judd will be in your office early tomorrow morning."

"I'll be there."

"Oh, and one more thing, Judge," Clint said.

"What's that?"

"I think you better find another place to have your fun."

Wilkie hesitated, then nodded and left.

Auggie appeared in the hall.

"Did we get what we wanted?" she asked.

"I think I did," Clint said. "We'll have to wait and see if you did."

"According to Jill," Auggie said, "she says he won't be back. But she also says if you come back, you can have a free poke."

"I'll keep that in mind."

Chapter Twenty-Six

Clint arrived at Ray Judd's office early the next morning, even before having breakfast. Judd was seated at his desk, looking glum.

"I talked to the judge yesterday," he said, as Clint entered. "Couldn't change his mind."

"I think you might have better luck if you go see him this morning," Clint said, sitting across from the lawyer.

Judd stared at Clint and asked, "What did you do?"

"Just a little blackmail," Clint said, "but as an officer of the court you probably don't want to hear about it."

"He's going to grant bail?"

"He is."

"How much?"

"That I don't know," Clint said.

"Can you cover it?"

"Between me and Rick, I'm sure we can," Clint said. "I told Wilkie you'd be there early."

Judd got hastily to his feet.

"I can't wait to see the look on his face when I walk in," he said.

"Join me for breakfast at Chino's afterward," Clint said. "I'll have coffee til you get there."

"And steak-and-eggs to celebrate!" Judd said.

"Agreed."

They left Judd's office together.

***

Clint ordered coffee after Chino seated him and told him they'd have two steak-and-egg-platters as soon as Ray Judd arrived.

"I'll put the order in when he gets here."

They didn't have to wait long before Judd came walking in and joined Clint at the table. Chino waved and went into the kitchen.

"That was fast," Clint said.

"You were right. He was waiting for me. His clerk ushered me right in, didn't even give me a time limit."

"And?"

Judd passed a sheet of paper over to Clint.

"He put it in writing."

Clint looked at the amount of bail.

"That's a lot."

"Think you can get him to reduce it?" Judd asked.

"That might be pressing my luck," Clint said. "Can I take this with me when I see Rick?"

"Sure," Judd said. "Let me know how soon you can get the money together."

Clint folded the bail notice and put it into his pocket. Chino came out of the kitchen with their breakfasts.

"I'll go and see Rick as soon as we're done here," he said.

"I'll wait at my office," Judd said. He cut into his steak and went on avidly. "You should've seen his face when I walked in . . ."

***

Clint entered the Sheriff's office and said, "Judge Wilkie sent me in to see Rick."

"Wilkie sent you?"

Clint nodded.

"I find that hard to believe."

"Well, believe this." He showed the lawman the bail notice.

Ritter whistled and handed it back.

"Can you get that much together?"

"That's what I'm here to talk with Rick about," Clint admitted. He took his gun out and handed it to the lawman. He thought that action was getting to be too much of a habit, and too easy to do.

Ritter walked him back and left him alone in front of Rick's cell.

"Take a look at this," he said, holding the bail slip out.

Rick took it, read it, and raised his eyebrows at Clint. "How did you get him to agree to this?"

"You don't want to know," Clint said. "Can you cover it? If you can't, I can go to the bank—"

"Don't worry about it," Rick said. "I don't have to cover it. I can get my bank to do it."

"The bank will put that money up?"

"Believe me," Rick said, "they don't want my place closing." He handed the slip back. "Just go to the bank and see the manager, Lester Savage."

"Savage?"

"I know, but he looks like a banker. He'll probably come up with the money right away, so I should be out of here this afternoon."

"I'll get right on it," Clint said.

"And Clint . . ."

"Yeah?"

"I don't know what you did," Rick said, "but thank you."

Chapter Twenty-Seven

Lester Savage did, indeed, look like a banker: a small man wearing a three-piece suit with a watch chain hanging from one vest pocket.

He raised his eyebrows as he looked at the amount on the bail slip.

"My word."

"Can you cover it?" Clint asked. He and Ray Judd were seated across from the bank manager's desk.

"Uh, um," Savage stammered, playing with his eyeglasses, bouncing them up-and-down on the bridge of his nose. "Um, yes, the bank can cover it for Mr. Hartman. But . . ."

"But what?"

Savage looked at Clint.

"Is he guilty?"

"Of course, he's not guilty," Judd said.

"And can you assure me he won't run?"

"Of course, I can," Clint said, "but why do you need my assurance? You know Rick Hartman better than you know me, or Mr. Judd, here."

"That's true," the bank manager said, "although I do know who Mr. Judd is. I've seen him around town."

"Then there shouldn't be a problem," Clint said.

"All right, I'll get the money ready, but as you say, I don't know you very well. I can't give it to you."

"You won't have to," Clint said. "Mr. Judd's his lawyer, and he's here to pick it up. And you have that bail slip, signed by Judge Wilkie."

"Yes, all right, Savage said. "It'll take me about an hour."

Clint and Judd stood up.

"We'll wait out front," Clint said.

"Very well."

They left the manager's office, went out to the main part of the bank, where there were chairs and desks.

A teller came from behind his cage and said, "Mr. Savage says you can sit by that empty desk and wait." He pointed.

"Thank you," Judd said.

After they were seated, Judd looked around, saw that they were attracting some attention.

"I don't have a gun," he said.

"That's all right," Clint said. "I do."

"If word gets out—"

"It won't," Clint said. "That's why we're sitting here, waiting."

"I hope you're right."

***

Half an hour later the bank manager, Savage, came out.

"Gentlemen," he said. "The money is ready."

They both stood and followed the manager into his office. The money was on his desk. Clint walked to the desk and filled the saddlebag he'd brought with the money.

"Will you sign here, Mr. Judd?" Savage asked.

The lawyer signed for the funds.

"I look forward to seeing Mr. Hartman a free man again," Savage said.

"Thank you, sir," Judd said.

Clint and Judd left the bank. Out front they stopped.

"Do you want the money?" Clint asked Judd.

"As I said," Judd replied, "I don't have a gun. Will you come with me to the courthouse?"

"Sure, I will," Clint said, "Let's get this done."

***

At the courthouse, the clerk said he would take the money.

"That's not a problem," Judd said, putting the saddle-bags on the young man's desk. "I'll just need a receipt to show the sheriff the bail's been paid."

"Of course," the clerk said, "but I'll need to count it."

Clint emptied the contents of the saddlebag onto the desk.

"Start counting," he said.

***

Clint and Judd entered the sheriff's office together.

"Gentlemen," Ritter said. "What can I do for you?"

"You can unlock the cell and let Rick Hartman out," Judd said, handing the lawman the receipt. "His bail has been paid."

The sheriff read the receipt. "So it seems."

He took his keys, entered the cell block and unlocked Rick's cell.

"You're a free man, Mr. Hartman," he said, then added, "for now."

Rick picked up his jacket and stepped out of the cell block. He faced both Clint and Judd.

"I thank you both for this," he said.

"Come on," Clint said, "let's get a drink."

Chapter Twenty-Eight

Shiloh set three beers up on the bar for Clint, Judd and Rick.

"Good to see you back, boss," he said.

"Good to be back."

They picked up their mugs and drank.

"What are you going to do first?" Shiloh asked.

"First, I'm going to take a bath," Rick said, "then some business. I'll try to regain some semblance of normalcy, until they come to get me for a trial."

"Hopefully," Judd said, "Clint can find out who really killed Ruth Bridges, and there won't be a trial."

"Well," Rick said, "so far he's done everything I could've asked of him."

"I'm not done, yet," Clint assured him.

Rick finished his beer and said, "I'm going to take that bath."

He shook hands with both men and went upstairs.

Judd turned to Clint.

"Well, you did it," he said. "I'm impressed."

"Like I told Rick," Clint said. "I'm not done, yet. Shiloh, two more beers."

***

Judge Wilkie looked up from his desk as Sheriff Ritter entered his chambers.

"Is he out?" he asked.

"Yessir," Ritter said. "There wasn't much else I could do once they showed me that receipt."

"That's all right," Wilkie said. "I understand."

"What now, Judge?"

"Just do your job, Sheriff," the Judge said. "Keep the peace. That's all you need to do."

"Yessir."

Ritter turned and left.

The Judge's clerk came in, then.

"I need Snow," the Judge said. "Find me Jack Snow."

"Yessir."

The clerk withdrew.

Moments later there was a knock on his door and the clerk reentered.

"What is it?" Wilkie asked.

"The mayor's here, sir. He'd like to see you."

"Send him in."

The clerk withdrew, and Mayor Ted Buchanan entered the office.

"Ted," Wilkie said, "have a seat."

Buchanan sat down.

"What's going on, Judge?" the Mayor asked. "I just heard that Rick Hartman's free."

"Temporarily," Wilkie said. "He's out on bail."

"Bail? I thought you weren't granting bail?"

"I changed my mind," Wilkie said. "But I made it a high amount."

"And he paid it?"

"In cash." Wilkie reached down, picked up the saddlebag Clint Adams had left, and dropped it on his desk with a heavy thud.

"What are you going to do with it?"

"It goes into the war chest," Wilkie said. "You want to get reelected next year, don't you?"

"You know I do."

"Well, that's going to take cash."

"And it's going to take Rick Hartman not being around to decide to run against me."

"I haven't heard anything about him having political ambitions."

"Neither have I," Buchanan said, "but the fact remains, he's the only man in town who could beat me. All he'd have to do is decide to run."

"Well," Wilkie said, "that's not going to happen."

"And what about the Gunsmith?" the Mayor asked.

"You leave him to me," Wilkie said. "He's made a big mistake."

"What's that?"

"He's made an enemy of me."

***

When they left the courthouse Clint and Judd went to the lawyer's office.

"My guess is," Judd said, "now that Rick is out, the Judge will set a trial date."

"How soon?"

"Pretty soon," Judd said. "I'll have to be ready, just in case we actually do go to trial."

"Then I better get to work and make sure that doesn't happen," Clint said.

"More questions?" Judd asked.

"Yes," Clint said, "I just have to figure out who to ask."

Chapter Twenty-Nine

Clint decided that the person he should talk to next was Rick Hartman. He gave Rick time to have his bath, and then found him in his office.

"Back to work already," Clint said, as he entered.

"Nobody's going to do it for me," Rick said. "Have a seat."

Clint sat across from his friend.

"You know," Rick said, sitting back, "it feels real good to be out. I've got to thank you, again."

"Don't thank me until we get you completely out of this," Clint said. "I've talked to a lot of your competitors over in the red light district."

"Like who?"

"August Dewey, Dean Macklin, some others."

"Those would be the main two," Rick said. "What'd they have to say?"

"That they didn't know Ruth Bridges and had no reason to kill her."

"Not even to frame me?"

"That's just it," Clint said. "They claim they have no reason to frame you. They don't want you out of business."

"Competitors who don't want me out of business?" Rick asked.

"They claim there's room for everybody," Clint said. "They say your place is important to the town."

"And you believe them?"

"I believe they didn't kill Ruth," Clint said. "The other stuff . . . well, you tell me."

"I never would've thought that was their feeling about this place. You never know."

"I also talked with Harlan Kellog and his foreman, Tim Crockett," Clint said. "Seems they were both sweet on Ruth, but like everybody else, deny having anything to do with killing her."

"Kellog proposed to her," Rick said. "She told me that. I didn't know about Crockett, though."

"Apparently, neither did Kellog, and Crockett wants to keep it that way," Clint said. "He doesn't want his boss to know."

"I don't blame him," Rick said. "Ruth told me Harlan was very upset when she turned him down."

"Really? That's not what he told me."

"What did he say?"

"That he thought she'd make a proper wife, but when she turned him down, he just moved on."

"That doesn't sound like the Harlan Kellog I know," Rick said. "He's never just moved on. He usually makes people pay for not doing things his way."

"Are you saying you think he killed her? How well do you know him?"

"He's been in my place plenty of times," Rick said. "And no, I don't think he killed her. He was more likely to buy her building and put her out of business. That's how he gets his way."

"I've got to tell you, Rick, I'm not sure which way to go," Clint said. "Was Ruth the target, or just a way to get to you?"

"I'd say me," Rick said. "Ruth was a fine woman, Clint. I don't know why anyone would want to kill her, unless it was to get to me."

"And that's not your ego talking?"

Rick leaned forward.

"I have an ego, that's for sure," he said, "but no, that's not my ego talking. The woman didn't offend anybody."

"I heard men were after her," Clint said. "That's got to mean some women didn't like her."

"So you're thinking a woman might've killed her?" Rick asked. He thought that over, then shook his head. "Women don't slit throats."

"She would if she wanted to blame the murder on someone else," Clint said.

"So now we're talking about a woman who wants me to go down for murder?"

"Who were you seeing before Ruth?" Clint asked.

"Her name was Naomi," Rick said. "She worked for me, but left town just before I met Ruth. No reason for her to want me in prison."

"Why'd she leave?"

"She said it was time, that's all," Rick said.

Clint nodded.

"Women come and go, Clint," Rick said.

"Oh, I know that."

"And speaking of women," Rick went on, "have you seen your lady barber?"

"Mel Jones," Clint said. "I have seen her, yes, but I haven't had the time to spend with her."

"Well, you do now," Rick said. "I'm out."

"And we've got to try and make sure you stay out," Clint said.

"Take tonight off, Clint," Rick said. "Spend time with Miss Jones. And tomorrow, we can start working on proving me innocent."

"Actually," Clint said, "that doesn't sound like a bad idea."

Chapter Thirty

"Your honor?"

Judge Wilkie looked up from his desk at his clerk, standing in the doorway of his chambers.

"Yes, what is it?"

"It's Jack Snow, sir."

"What about him? Did you find him?"

"Yes, I did."

"And?"

"He won't come here, sir," the clerk said. "He said if you want to see him, you have to go to him."

"And where would that be?"

"The Salvation Saloon, sir, in the red light district," the clerk said. "Four o'clock."

"The one run by the priest?"

"Yes, sir."

Wilkie frowned.

"That's an odd place."

"Yes, sir."

"All right," Wilkie said. "Fine. Thank you."

"Yes, sir."

The clerk left and closed the door.

Judge Wilkie opened the top drawer of his desk, looked at the short-barreled Colt revolver he kept there, and then closed it again.

***

Clint left Rick's place and walked to the barber shop, where Mel was busy cutting a man's hair. She looked out the window at him and smiled, then held up five fingers and pointed at the clock on the wall. She wanted him to come back at five o'clock. He nodded, waved, and walked on.

Next, he went to Ruth Bridge's store to talk to Lily again. The young girl was with a customer, and he waited until the woman left with her purchase.

"Can I help you, Mr. Adams?" she asked. "Or have you come to tell me you found something?"

"No, I haven't found anything, yet," Clint said. "But I did want to tell you that Rick Hartman has been released on bail."

"A murderer? And he's out?" She seemed alarmed.

"He's not a murderer," Clint said. "That's what I'm trying to prove."

"W-what do you want me to do?" she asked. "I gave you the names you wanted."

"I just came to ask you again, did Ruth ever mention someone she was afraid of? Or anyone who threatened her?"

Lily thought for a few moments, then said, "She did once mention a man named Snow."

***

Judge Wilkie entered the Salvation Saloon. The short-barreled Colt from his desk was tucked into his belt. He assumed at least half of the patrons in the place had appeared in his courtroom and would recognize him. He also assumed Jack Snow, by insisting they meet there, was testing him.

He walked to the bar, where the bartender with the clerical collar regarded him with no expression. Likewise, Judge Wilkie regarded the crucifix over the bar in the same manner.

"Judge Wilkie," he said. "To what do we owe this visit? Seeking salvation?"

"If I was," Wilkie said, "it wouldn't be here. I'm meeting someone, so just let me have a beer and mind your own business, Parson."

The bartender set a frothy beer down in front of the Judge and said, "I answer to Father Elvis."

"Yes, right," Wilkie said. "I'll remember that."

Wilkie turned with his beer in hand and regarded the room. Snow didn't seem to be at the bar or at a table.

"Snow," Father Elvis said.

"What?" Judge Wilkie said, turning.

"You're looking for Jack Snow."

"How would you know that?"

"He told me you'd be here," Father Elvis said. "He's in the back room, through that green curtain."

"How do I know what's waiting back there," the Judge asked.

"You came here alone, so you're not worried about being bushwhacked," Elvis said. "Besides, all who come here are welcome in the house of the Lord."

"Even a killer like Jack Snow?"

"You have sent men to the gallows, Judge?" Father Elvis said. "Does that make you a killer?"

"I don't hang them myself."

"So you have others do your killing for you," the priest said.

"Legally."

"You'll forgive me for giving more credence to a man who does his own killing."

"A priest who supports a killer?" the Judge said.

Father Elvis pressed his hands together and said, "All are forgiven, here."

Wilkie headed for the green curtain, beer in hand.

Chapter Thirty-One

"Snow?" Clint asked.

"Jack Snow," she said.

"Who is he?"

"A hired gun," Lily said. "I thought you would've heard of him."

"No," Clint said. "He knew Ruth?"

"She said he approached her on the street one day," Lily said. "Actually, she was 'accosted.'"

"And she turned him away?"

Lily nodded.

"She said he didn't like it one bit."

"Jack Snow, huh?" He'd have to ask Sheriff Ritter, or Rick, about the man. "Have you ever seen him?"

"No, never."

"All right, Lily," Clint said. "Thanks."

He started for the door, then stopped.

"Just out of curiosity, do you intend to keep the store open?"

"As long as I can," she said. "Until somebody tells me I can't."

"Well, good luck."

He left.

***

Judge Wilkie went through the green curtain into the back room. Jack Snow was seated at a round, wooden poker table, shuffling a deck of cards. Wilkie couldn't see them, but he knew the man was wearing a pearl-handled Colt on his hip.

"Hello, Judge."

Wilkie knew one of the reasons he didn't command more respect from Snow was that the gunman was older than he was. Being a young judge made it hard to gain the respect he felt he deserved, so he had to do it in other ways.

"Snow."

"Have a seat."

Wilkie sat across from the gunman, who had a beer at his elbow.

"What's on your mind?" Snow asked.

"Do you know that Clint Adams is in town?"

Snow nodded.

"He comes to Labyrinth a lot," Snow said, "although we've never been here at the same time."

"Well, you are now," Wilkie said. "And you know what that means?"

"What?"

"You can elevate your reputation."

"By killin' the Gunsmith?" Snow asked.

"That's right."

"For you?"

"No," Wilkie said. "I'm not paying you to kill a man."

"Then what are you sayin'?" Snow asked.

"I'm saying," Wilkie explained, "that you will not be prosecuted for killing this man."

"What if I shoot 'im in the back?" Snow asked.

"I don't care where you shoot him."

"To—how did you put it?—elevate my reputation, I'd have to beat him fair and square, in the street."

"That's up to you, Snow," Wilkie said. "I'm just giving you some information."

"I see."

Wilkie sipped his beer and stood up, leaving the rest of it on the table.

"Do you wanna know when it's done?"

"Oh, I'll know," Wilkie said. "Everybody will know."

He turned and walked out.

***

Clint meant his next stop to be Rick's Place, but walking down the street he saw Sheriff Ritter coming toward him.

"Not looking for me, are you?" Clint asked.

"Just makin' my rounds," Ritter said.

"I heard a name," Clint said. "I wonder if you can tell me anything about him."

"What's the name?"

"Snow, Jack Snow."

"Let's just say, if you run into him, only one of you will walk away."

"He's like that, huh?"

"He's like that," Ritter said.

"I just heard something about him," Clint said, "thought I'd talk to him."

"If you want him to talk," Ritter said, "I'd suggest you get the drop on him, first."

"I'll keep that in mind," Clint said. "Thanks for the tip."

"Any time," Ritter said. "Anything I can do to keep bodies from litterin' my streets."

The sheriff continued on his rounds, and Clint headed for Rick's.

Chapter Thirty-Two

"Jack Snow," Rick said.

"That's the name."

"Oh, I know him," Rick said.

They were sitting at Rick's table with a beer each.

"What's he got to do with this?"

"Looks like he was also after Ruth Bridges," Clint said.

"She never told me that."

"She probably didn't want you to get killed," Clint said.

"That would've been like her," Rick said. "So what are you going to do?"

"I'd like to talk to him, but the sheriff says he's not the talkative type," Clint said. "That is, unless I can get the drop on him."

"My money would be on you," Rick said.

"Something else occurs to me," Clint said.

"What's that?"

"If you do end up going to trial, we don't have to prove you didn't do it, we'd just have to show that somebody else could've."

"Reasonable doubt."

"Right."

"I guess that's something we'd have to talk with Mr. Judd about," Hartman said.

"That's what I was thinking," Clint said. "I'll talk to him about it tomorrow."

"Good," Rick said. "I'm going to continue working, unless you come and tell me you need me."

"I think the best thing for you to do is stay out of sight," Clint said. "There's no point in flaunting the fact that you're free to walk the streets . . . for now."

"Agreed."

Clint stood up.

"Where are you off to?" Rick asked.

"I think somebody suggested I should see a barber."

***

Mel Jones was waiting for him when he arrived at her empty barber shop.

"You're five minutes late," she said. "I thought you were going to stand me up."

"I'd never do that."

"I would've understood," she assured him. "I mean, you're trying to prove your friend innocent."

"Well," Clint said, "I got him out of jail, and he's safely at home, where I told him to stay. That gives me some time . . ."

"Time for what?" she asked.

"Time to spend with you."

"For a haircut?" she asked.

"Why not?" he asked. "For a start."

She ushered him into her chair and covered him with a sheet.

***

The three men met again.

"Why are we here now?" Third asked.

"Just to go over everything," First said. "Rick Hartman is out on bail."

"And how did that happen?" Second asked.

"Somehow Clint Adams arranged it," First said.

"Wilkie doesn't give in easily," Second said. "What did Adams do . . . blackmail him?"

"That's a possibility," First said.

"So here we sit," Second said, "talking and not doing a damn thing about it."

"Well," First said, "it just so happens I have a plan . . .

***

Mel cut Clint's hair, careful to stroke his neck and face, brushing up against him, every chance she got. At one point she was standing in front of him, between his legs, putting the finishing touches on.

"There," she said, "we're done."

"Done?" Clint said, reaching for her, "we haven't even started, yet."

He pulled her to him and kissed her deeply. She dropped her scissors to the floor and wrapped her arms around him. They kissed passionately for a long time before she drew back and removed the sheet covering him. His shorn locks went flying to the floor.

Outside, darkness had fallen.

"Wait," she said, pushing away from him, "I have to douse the lamp."

She blew the flame out, and then returned to the chair, started unbuttoning his shirt.

"Now nobody can see us from outside," she assured him.

Chapter Thirty-Three

She tossed his shirt aside, and when she got his boots off, started on his trousers.

"I know, I know," she said, "we'll hang the gun right here, so you can reach it." She hung the gunbelt on the side of the chair. "See?"

Clint looked out the window, saw an older couple walk past, arm-in-arm.

"You sure they can't see us from out there?" he asked.

"I'm positive," she said, pulling off his pants. "I'll show you."

She got on her knees in front of the chair and took his already hard cock into her mouth. She bobbed her head a few times, then released him for a moment.

"Would I do this if I thought we could be seen?"

He was about to reply when she took him into her mouth again, shutting him up.

She took her time wetting him fully, gripping his thighs with her nails then stroking his testicles with her fingertips. She moaned as she felt his cock swell to bursting, and then abruptly allowed him to pop out of her mouth.

She got to her feet, stepped back and undressed before him. When she was naked, a shaft of light from outside, came through the window and illuminated her torso. He thought if anyone passed the window at that moment, they would have gotten a sight.

She went to him then, crawled up onto his lap, pressed her breasts against his face, lifted her hips and sat right down on his cock, taking it deep inside of her. He slid his hands beneath her to cup her fleshy buttocks, began to lift her and then let her drop down on him.

"Oh yes," she breathed, as he kissed and bit her breasts. He had a sudden flash of memory of being with Auggie Dewey, whose body was very similar to Mel's. Both women were the type he preferred, lovely, sweet smelling, with an abundance of passion and flesh.

His attention came back to the woman who was bouncing on him now. Luckily, her barber chair was attached to the floor, or it would have been traveling across the room.

"Mel," he said, "we need a bed."

"Later," she gasped into his ear, "right now this is what we've got and I'm going to make the most of it."

They had made love in his chair the first time they met, and he was convinced that she actually preferred it to a bed.

"All right, then," he said, and started to heave upward each time she came down, giving as good as he was getting . . .

***

Judge Wilkie sat in the den of his two-story house and poured himself a whiskey. He realized he couldn't go back to the Princess Pleasure Palace. Oh, he could, but then he'd have to go up against Auggie Dewey, and didn't relish that thought. She was a tough woman, tougher than most of the men in town.

There were other bordellos in town. He'd find one that had the kind of women he needed. On this evening, however, he was more concerned with what would happen when Jack Snow went against Clint Adams. He knew how fast Snow was but had only heard stories about the speed of the Gunsmith. The man was considered a legend, but that was what happened when people only heard stories. Clint Adams would have to prove he was the Gunsmith. Or he was going to prove he wasn't.

And Judge Wilkie wanted to be there to see it.

***

Jack Snow sat in the Salvation Saloon, also drinking whiskey, also thinking about Clint Adams. Snow knew he was fast. He had put more than a dozen men in the ground proving it. He had only heard stories about the Gunsmith, had never seen the man in action nor did he know anyone who had. Killing the Gunsmith would be his crowning achievement, or trying would be the last thing he ever did with a gun in his hand.

For men like him and Clint Adams, that was how it was destined to end, with a bullet. In the past he had never spent any time talking with a man he intended to kill, but this might be different.

He looked up as the bartender with the clerical collar brought him another whiskey.

"Are you really a priest?" he asked.

"I really am," the man said. "Father Elvis, at your service. Do you want something else, my son? Absolution? Salvation, perhaps? Confession."

"I ain't a Catholic, Father," Snow said. "And even if I was, I don't think the Lord would forgive the things I done."

"The Lord is infinite in his mercy and the bounty of his forgiveness."

"That may be," Snow said, "but I would test that forgiveness for sure."

"Well," Father Elvis said, "I'm at your service, if you change your mind."

Snow picked up his fresh glass of whiskey and said, "Thank you, Father."

Chapter Thirty-Four

Later, they took their union to bed.

They left the barber shop and walked together to her house, went directly to the bedroom and to her bed.

They were lying side-by-side, catching their breath after making love again.

"I told you we needed a bed," he said.

"I don't know," she said. "I kind of like my chair."

"Why?"

She rolled over to look at him.

"When I'm cutting a man's hair," she said, "I think about what you and I do in that chair, and it makes me laugh inside. Once or twice I've laughed out loud, and the men think I just enjoy cutting their hair, which makes me laugh even more."

"You're an odd woman, Mel," Clint said. "Beautiful, smart, and very tasty . . . but odd."

"Why thank you, sir," she said. "I feel the same way about you. I guess that's what makes us such a good match." She must have seen something in his face, because hurriedly she added, "Don't think I'm proposing, though. I'm not looking to get married."

"That's good," Clint said. "Neither am I."

"Have you ever thought about it?" she asked. "Ever come close?"

"Once," he said.

"When?"

"A lot of years ago."

"What happened?"

"She died," Clint said. "She was killed."

Mel settled down on her back, again.

"I'm sorry I brought it up."

"That's okay," Clint said.

He sat up.

"You're leaving?"

"I need to get an early start in the morning," he said. "that means I need sleep." He looked at her, at her nude body. "I'm not going to get that here. I think we both know that."

"Well," she said, "you be sure to let me know if you want another haircut while you're in town."

Fully dressed and at the door, he turned and said, "Oh, you'll be the first to know."

***

He woke the next morning feeling both well-rested, and pleasantly fatigued. After a quick breakfast in the hotel, he went to Raymond Judd's office, found the man seated behind his desk.

"So, what's on the agenda today?" Judd asked.

"For you, I think you ought to talk with Rick," Clint said. "You'll find him over at his place."

"And you?" Judd asked. "What are your plans?"

"I'm going to find Jack Snow," Clint said. "See what he has to say."

"From what I've heard, he doesn't usually say much," Judd said. "He lets his gun do the talking."

"Oh, I think he'll talk to me."

"Why?"

"For one thing, he'll want to make sure I am who I say I am," Clint said. "If and when he kills me, he'll want to be sure he killed the Gunsmith."

"I hope you're right," Judd said. "And I mean about him talking to you, not killing you."

"Yeah, I hope so, too," Clint said. "I'll check in with you later."

"I'll either be here or at Rick's Place," Judd said. "We've got to get our strategies straight."

"And hopefully," Clint said, "you won't need them."

***

Clint entered the Salvation Saloon, which had just opened.

"Mr. Adams," Father Elvis said. "Welcome."

"Father."

"A beer?" Father Elvis asked. "I know it's early, but this is a saloon, after all."

"Sure, why not?" Clint said. "I'll have a beer."

"What brings you here this time of day?"

"I've been to a few places," Clint said. "I'm looking for a man named Jack Snow."

"Why would you be looking for a sinner like Jack Snow?"

"How do you know he's a sinner?" Clint asked.

"He was here last night," Father Elvis said. "I offered him absolution, but he refused."

"I guess he's not worried about paying for his sins in the afterlife," Clint said.

"And you Mr. Adams?" Father Elvis said. "What about paying for your sins?"

"My time will come, Father," Clint said. "You say Snow was here last night?"

"He was."

"Do you know where he is now?"

"I don't."

"Do you think he'll come back here today?"

"I think so," Father Elvis said. "I think he prefers this place to any of the others."

"What about the pleasure palaces?"

"You might find him there," the priest said. "But if you find him, one of you will die, no?"

"It's possible."

"Then I wish you would both seek absolution before that happens," Father Elvis said.

"When I find him," Clint said, "I'll tell him you said that."

Chapter Thirty-Five

Clint entered Sheriff Ritter's office and said, "You're the law. Where can I find Jack Snow?"

"How would I know?" Ritter asked.

"Don't you keep track of men like him and me?" Clint asked.

"I couldn't have told anyone where you were last night or this mornin', either," Ritter said. "Besides, why would you want to find him? You're just gonna have to kill 'im."

"I just want to talk to him," Clint said.

"Well, good luck with that," the lawman said. "From what little I know of him, he's not a talker."

"That's what I've been hearing," Clint said.

"You might be interested to know that Judge Wilkie has started to interview for a jury," Ritter said. "Once he has them, he'll put your friend Hartman on trial."

"Why are you telling me this?"

"I just thought you should know, that's all."

"Thanks, Sheriff," Clint said, and left the office.

***

Clint's options were to keep searching for Jack Snow or go tell Rick and Judd that Wilkie was assembling his jury. He decided the lawyer needed to know, so he went to Rick's Place.

Even though it was too early for the place to be open, the front door wasn't locked, so Clint entered. He found Rick and Judd sitting at a table, Judd drinking coffee while Rick ate breakfast.

"That was fast," Judd said, as Clint entered. "You just left my office a little while ago."

"It's been a couple of hours," Clint said. "You fellas finished with your strategy?"

"Took a break for breakfast," Rick said. "At least, I did."

"I ate before I came here," Judd said. "What brings you by so early? Find Snow?"

"No," Clint said, "but I did hear something." He told them what sheriff Ritter said about Judge Wilkie assembling a jury.

"Looks like all of a sudden he's in a hurry," Judd commented.

"Things haven't been going his way," Clint pointed out. "He probably thinks he needs to make a move."

"Before I bolt and head for Mexico," Rick added.

Judd looked at Rick quickly.

"Is that something you're considering?" he asked.

"No," Rick said, "I was kidding, Judd. I'm going to beat this thing legally."

Judd seemed to relax, then looked at Clint.

"I thought your plan was to find Jack Snow?"

"It was, but I came across this information and thought you should know."

"Why don't you just let Snow find you?" Rick suggested. "With the both of you in town, he won't pass up the chance at you."

"That's true enough, but with Wilkie getting his jury together, I need to get to Snow before the judge puts you before a jury."

"I suppose that makes sense," Rick said.

"You know, when Wilkie's ready he's going to send Sheriff Ritter to bring you in again," Clint said, "but if he can't find you—"

"Forget that," Rick said. "I'm not going to run, and I'm not going to hide, either."

"What if Wilkie's got it in for you and is planning to find you guilty no matter what?" Clint asked.

"He's a judge," Judd said. "He's got to go with the evidence, and I just don't see that there is any."

"So you don't think they *can* find Rick guilty?" Clint asked.

"Well," Judd said, "with a jury you never can tell, but . . ."

". . . but I better keep looking," Clint finished.

"Maybe Jack Snow will make a good alternative," Judd said, "and give us some reasonable doubt."

"The only thing is, if Snow killed her, it probably would've been with a gun, not a knife."

"So that puts us back where we started," Rick said.

"Yes," Clint said, "me out there, and you in here."

"That never occurred to me," Judd said. "If somebody wants Rick out of the way and can't get him convicted, they might just try to kill him."

"Probably as a last resort," Clint said, "but let's keep him inside, anyway."

"I don't know," Rick said. "That sure sounds like hiding to me."

"Let's just say it's being cautious and leave it at that," Clint said. "What do you say?"

"Sure," Rick said. "I suppose there's no point in being stupid about it."

"Agreed," Judd said.

"Then I'll leave the two of you to your strategizing, and get back out there, myself."

Chapter Thirty-Six

Clint wasn't sure about his next move. Going over to the red light district to look for Snow, he'd be finding a lot of those places not open yet for business. He decided to go back to his hotel to have a drink, or just a cup of coffee, and give some more thought to what his actions should be. When he reached the lobby, he went into the dining room and not the bar. He was having a cup of coffee when the desk clerk rushed in.

"This came for you a little while ago, sir," the man said, handing Clint a note.

"Who brought it in?"

"I don't know," the clerk said. "It was just on my desk."

"Okay, thanks."

As the clerk left, Clint unfolded the note. It said:

IF YOU WANT PROOF THAT RICK HARTMAN DIDN'T KILL RUTH BRIDGES, MEET ME AT THE STOCKYARDS AT 11:00 P.M. It was unsigned.

Clint wouldn't have given it much thought except that it called for a meeting at the same place Rick was called to the night Ruth was killed. And nobody showed up that night.

Maybe this would be different.

***

Clint was in the stockyards at ten forty-five. He took cover behind one of the stalls and waited to see who would arrive. When a man did appear, walking slowly and looking around, Clint continued to wait. By eleven fifteen he didn't see or sense anyone else, so he stepped out into the open.

"Here," he said.

The man turned quickly, startled, then relaxed.

"Mr. Adams?"

"That's right."

The man approached him.

"That's far enough," he said.

The man stopped.

"We're quite alone," he assured Clint.

It was dark, but he could see that the man was middle-aged, well dressed, not tall.

"Who are you?" he asked.

"That's not important," the man said. "What is important is that I know Rick Hartman didn't kill Ruth Bridges."

"The question is, will you testify to that?"

"No," the man said. "I can't."

"Then what good are you to me?"

"At least you know your friend's not a murderer," the man answered.

"I didn't need you to tell me that," Clint said. "I know Rick Hartman's not a killer."

"Well then," the man said, "I've risked my life here for nothing." He looked around.

"Relax," Clint said. "Like you said, there's nobody else here. Why don't you tell me why you asked me to meet you here? Really?"

The man shifted his feet nervously.

"I don't like what's happening here," he said, finally.

"And just what is happening here?" Clint asked.

"Well," the man said, "it's not justice, that's for sure."

"Can you—listen, what can I call you?"

"Why don't you just call me . . . Three."

"Three?"

The man nodded.

"Well, Mr. Three—"

"Just Three."

"All right," Clint said. "Three it is. "Do you happen to know who did kill Ruth Bridges?"

"No," Three said, "I only know that Rick Hartman is supposed to take the blame."

"And Judge Wilkie's in on it?"

"Of course."

"Do you know if Jack Snow killed her?"

149

"All I know is that he didn't do it," Three said.

"Are you sure of that?"

"Dead sure."

"All right," Clint said, "then I only have to worry about Snow trying to kill me."

"I can't help you with that," Three said. "That's going to be between you and him."

"So far," Clint said, "you haven't really helped me with anything."

"I'm sorry," Three said. "I'm doing what I can."

"Then tell me something I can use," Clint said.

Three looked around again, then lowered his voice.

"You've seen what's new in Labyrinth since the last time you were here, haven't you?"

"You mean the red light district?"

"Have you gone past the red light district?"

"There's more?" Clint asked.

"There is."

"So what is it that's on the other side of the red light district?" Clint asked.

Three leaned in and said, "Chinatown."

Chapter Thirty-Seven

Clint burst into Judd's office the next morning and glared at the man.

"There's a Chinatown in Labyrinth?" he demanded.

"There is."

"And nobody thought to tell me that?"

"What's the point?"

"That woman's throat was cut," Clint said. "China-men use knives."

"So now you think a Chinaman killed her?"

"I think it's another possibility," Clint said. "I'm going over there and have a look. What am I walking into? How big is the area?"

"Not big," Judd said. "A couple of laundries, a dry goods store, a couple of small restaurants—if you can call what they eat food—and some Chinese pleasure palaces."

"Any saloons?"

"Probably."

"You don't know?"

"I don't spend much time there," Judd said.

"Do you do your own laundry?"

"Well . . . all right, yeah, I take my laundry over there," Judd admitted, "but that's about it."

"Christ . . ."

"Why don't you get mad at your friend Hartman?" Judd asked. "He didn't tell you, either."

"You and me, we're supposed to be working on getting him free," Clint said. "All I need from him is to stay inside until we do."

"So what are you going to do in Chinatown?" Judd asked.

"The same thing I've been doing in the red light district," Clint answered. "Ask questions."

"Have you dealt with Chinese before?"

"Yes," Clint said, "in San Francisco, Denver and New York."

"Well, this isn't any of those places," Judd said.

"There have also been Chinatowns in Tombstone, Deadwood and Wichita, among others."

"Still maybe you should take the law with you."

"You know," Clint said, "you might have a point there."

***

"You want me to do what?" Sheriff Ritter asked.

"You heard me," Clint said, "I want you to come with me to Chinatown."

"You got some laundry you want done?"

"No, but I've got some questions I'd like answered."

"Why the sudden interest in Chinatown?" Ritter asked.

"Because I just found out Labyrinth has a Chinatown," Clint said. "This town is growing much faster than I ever imagined."

"You got that right," Ritter said. "Is this part of your attempt to prove Hartman innocent?"

"It is," Clint said. "So, are you coming?"

"Why not?" Ritter said. "I happen to like Chinese food."

***

Judd was right. The Chinatown area was not large. As they crossed the imaginary line from the red light district, Clint could see almost everything—the laundries, a saloon, a couple of restaurants, and a dry goods store.

"This is it?" he asked Ritter.

"Yep," the lawman said, "all of it. Not much, is there?"

As they walked, women washing and hanging laundry turned to look at them.

"The one thing you can't see is behind the dry goods store," Ritter said. "The whorehouse."

"Let's try the saloon," Clint said.

"Why not?"

There were no batwing doors, just a traditional door with colored glass. Clint turned the knob and they entered, drawing the attention of the few Chinamen who were seated inside, drinking. No one was standing at the bar, except for a bartender.

"Clint," Ritter said, "this is Fong. He owns the place. There's no name on the outside, but everyone knows it as Fong's."

"Mr. Fong," Clint said.

"Fong, this is Clint Adams."

"It is a pleasure," Fong said. He was a portly man with black hair, but his face was passive and did not betray his age, which could have been anything from forty to sixty.

"We'll have two Baijiu," Ritter said.

"Right away."

"Baijiu?" Clint asked.

"A Chinese whiskey made from rice," Ritter said. "It could be strong or light."

"How does he know which one to give us?" Clint asked.

"He'll give us what he wants."

When Fong returned, he set two glasses of clear, aromatic liquid in front of them.

"Baijiu," he said.

"Down the hatch," Ritter said.

He and Clint drank the liquor, and Clint immediately started coughing as it burned its way down.

"Wow," he said, looking at Fong, "what's the light one like?"

"That was the light one," Fong said.

Chapter Thirty-Eight

Clint and Ritter had another glass of Baijiu while Fong stood there and watched.

"Why are you here, Sheriff?" he asked. Clint noticed that Fong spoke almost perfect English.

"Mr. Adams is lookin' for somethin'," Ritter said. "I just came along to smooth the way. Oh, and to have some Chinese food."

Fong looked at Clint.

"What are you looking for?"

"A man who kills," Clint said, "and prefers a knife."

"There are many men in Labyrinth who kill with a knife," Fong said.

"I'm looking for a Chinese man."

"Many of those, as well."

"Are there any who would hire out?" Clint asked.

"You want to find a hired Chinese killer?" Fong asked.

"I'm just curious," Clint said, "about whether or not there are any."

"Look around," Fong said. "Talk to these men and see if any of them would like the job."

"I'm not looking to hire a killer," Clint said, "I just want to see if it's possible."

"For the right amount of money, anything is possible," Fong said.

"Is that what you wanted to hear?" Ritter asked.

"Thank you, Mr. Fong," Clint said.

"It is just Fong," the bartender said.

Clint turned to Ritter.

"You said something about Chinese food?"

***

Sheriff Ritter took Clint into one of the same restaurants they had passed, where he ordered them dumplings, shrimp fried rice and chicken chow mein.

"You had Chinese food before?" the lawman asked.

"Once or twice," Clint said. "And you've been here to Chinatown before?"

"In the course of my job," Ritter said, "and sometimes for laundry or food."

"Fong knew you."

"Well, yeah, I've been in his place for a drink a few times."

Two waiters came, carrying platters of food that they covered the table with. The lawman also ordered hot tea for both of them.

As they started eating, Ritter asked, "Did you get what you were looking for?"

"Not really," Clint said. "I mean, Judd can talk about Chinatown in court, but I don't know if a jury will believe that a Chinaman killed Ruth Bridges."

"What about your theory regarding Jack Snow?"

"It wasn't so much a theory as it was a hunch," Clint said. "Now I just want to talk to the man."

"So you're figurin' Judd will give the jury Snow and a Chinaman and that'll give you reasonable doubt?"

"No," Clint said, "I'm still hoping to keep this from going to court, at all."

"To do that, you got to find the real killer."

"That's what I'm looking for here," Clint said.

"I don't understand what put you on to Chinatown," Ritter said.

Clint decided not to tell the lawman about his meeting with "Three."

"I just heard somebody mention it," Clint said, "and I'd never heard about it before."

"It's probably the newest section in town," Ritter said, "which is why it ain't a big one . . . yet."

They continued to eat while Clint went over in his mind his meeting with "Three" the night before. After the man had said "Chinatown" he'd turned and hurried away. Clint thought about following him, but waited too long and the man disappeared into the darkness.

He thought he might tell Ritter about the meeting and describe the man. But in the end figured he could do that with Rick or Judd, who might be able to identify the stranger. He didn't know how closely Ritter would be working with Judge Wilkie when it came right down to it.

***

As the waiters came to the table to clean it off, one of them brushed against Clint. The man shoved something into his hand as Clint and Ritter stood to leave.

"We might as well head back," the lawman said.

"You go ahead," Clint said. "You've probably got work to do. I'll stay around here a while longer."

"You sure you wanna do that alone?" Ritter asked.

"I'll be fine," Clint assured him.

"All right," Ritter said. "It's your call."

The lawman headed off, and Clint waited until he was out of sight before he looked at the note in his hand.

Chapter Thirty-Nine

The note was written in barely legible script, but Clint got the message. Somebody wanted to meet him behind the restaurant, probably the waiter who gave him the note.

He stood in front of the restaurant until the sheriff was out of sight, then stepped into the dusty street and made his way around to the back. The aromas in front of the place had been appetizing, but the odors in the back were very different. There were overflowing garbage cans, as wells as ditches that had been dug and used for various disposals.

Clint wrinkled his nose and tried to stand as far away from the odors as he could. Before long, a man stuck his head out the back door, looked around, spotted him and came running over. It was their waiter.

"Fong say you look for blade man," the waiter said.

"I asked about it, yeah."

"You want blade man, I get you blade man," the waiter said. "You pay?"

"Yes, I'll pay," Clint said. "What's the man's name?"

"No name," the waiter said. "You pay, I get you blade man."

"I want his name," Clint said, "and I want to talk to him."

"Talk?"

"Yes, I'll pay to talk."

The waiter jabbed his chest with his thumb and said, "You pay Ling?"

"Yes," Clint said, "I'll pay Ling and the blade man."

"You come back later," Ling said, "you talk to blade man."

"When later?"

"Five o'clock."

"All right," Clint said, "five o'clock, right here."

Ling bowed to him, then turned and ran back to the restaurant. Clint left, vowing not to eat there, again.

***

"You did what?" Rick asked. "You went to the stock-yards alone after what happened to me?"

"Well, I wasn't going to have you go with me," Clint said, "especially after what happened last time, so yeah, I went alone. Anyway, the man showed up."

"Who was it?"

"He wouldn't give me a name," Clint said. "He told me to call him Three."

"What'd he look like?"

"Not tall, middle-aged, wearing a dark suit and hat, seemed the nervous type."

"That could match a few men," Rick said.

"Why would he want to be called Three?" Clint asked. "A number, not a name?"

"Wait a minute," Rick said, snapping his fingers. "There's a faction in town who started buying up property as soon as they got here."

"Who are they?" Clint asked. "What are their names?"

"Their names won't matter to you," Rick said, "but they call themselves The Three."

"Why?" Clint asked.

"The simple answer is that there are three of them," Rick said. "Three men who own half the businesses in town."

"And did they try to buy yours when they got here?" Clint asked.

"They did," Rick said. "I turned them down several times."

"And the description I gave you matches one of them?"

"It does," Rick said, "A man named John Gideon."

"Then I think I should go and talk to Mr. Gideon," Clint said.

"Maybe you should talk to him away from the other two, though," Rick suggested. "That means not at their offices, which are down the street."

"So where?"

"Well," Rick said, "they do business together, so they're usually in the office together, but once they leave, they seem to go their own ways."

"So they don't have supper together?"

"No."

Clint frowned.

"I've got to go back to Chinatown at five o'clock."

"They'll probably still be at supper when you're done," Rick said, "providing you don't get killed going to Chinatown alone."

"Do you know where they take their meals, these three?" Clint asked.

"No," Rick said, "but there are only a few places men like that would choose."

"All right," Clint said, "right after Chinatown."

"I think I should come with you."

"To Chinatown, or to checkout restaurants?"

"Both!"

"I don't think so, Rick," Clint said. "It's better for you to stay here, where you can be safe."

"Safe?" Rick asked. "I'm hiding to be safe?"

"All right, then," Clint said, "so you can stay out of trouble."

Chapter Forty

Clint returned to Chinatown to meet with the waiter, Ling. This time he was prepared for the smells behind the restaurant. Ling was waiting there for him.

"Ling," he said.

"You pay," the waiter said, "Ling get you blade man."

"You show me the blade man," Clint said, "and then I'll pay you."

Ling turned and waved, and another Chinaman appeared from behind the building. As they stood side-by-side he found he couldn't tell them apart, except that Chang was dressed better.

"This is him?" Clint asked.

"This Chang," Ling said. "He blade man." The waiter put out his hand. "You pay, two dollar."

Clint put a silver dollar into Ling's hand.

"One."

Ling looked at the coin in his hand, then closed it into a fist and nodded. He turned and entered the restaurant through the back door.

"You pay?" Chang said. "I kill."

"Do you kill women?" Clint asked.

The small man frowned.

"If you pay more, I kill woman." He showed Clint his knife.

"Did you kill a woman recently?"

"You pay," Chang said, "I kill."

"I'm asking you if somebody paid you to kill a woman named Ruth Bridges?"

"Bridges?" Chang asked. "The woman Rick Hartman killed?"

Suddenly, Chang spoke better English.

"You're educated," Clint said.

Chang smiled.

"Can we get away from these smells?" Clint asked.

Chang nodded.

"Follow me," he said.

He led Clint to the street in front of the restaurant, then led him to Fong's saloon.

"Chang," Fong greeted, "and Mr. Adams. Baijiu?"

"Yes," Clint said, and Chang nodded.

Fong poured them each a glass.

"I did not kill Ruth Bridges," Chang said to Clint in perfect English.

"Do you know who did?"

"No."

"Can you find out?"

"Are you asking me if I can find out if a Chinese killed her?" Chang asked.

"Yes."

"Why would I help you?" Chang asked.

"I'll pay you."

"To deliver a guilty man?"

"If you know there is one," Clint said. "But if you tell me you're dead sure a Chinaman didn't kill her, I'll still pay you."

"What makes you think I would know, or be able to find out?" Chang asked.

"She was killed with a knife," Clint said. "I believe a white man would've shot her or beaten her to death."

"White men don't use knives?"

"In this case," Clint said, "you tell me."

Clint put some coins on the bar.

"That much again when you give me my answer."

Chang drank down his Baijiu and said, "Agreed. Meet me here again tomorrow night."

Clint drank his and left.

***

According to Rick, there were three restaurants in Labyrinth that the Three would eat in. Usually, they ate in them separately.

Clint checked two of them, peering in the windows, and didn't see the man he knew as Three. One or Two

166

could have been in there, but there was no way for him to know that. And at the moment he was interested in Mr. Three.

At the third restaurant, the Bonanza Steakhouse, he peered in the window and saw the man sitting alone, eating. As he entered, a man in a suit approached him.

"Mr. Adams, isn't it?" he asked.

"That's right."

"Can I get you a table, sir?"

"I'm joining a friend of mine," Clint said. "He's right there."

"Ah, Mr. Gideon?"

"That's right."

"Very well. Enjoy your meal."

"Thanks."

Clint walked across the dining room to Gideon Three's table. The man saw him coming and started to rise, looking panicked.

"Sit back down and finish your meal," Clint said. "We're going to talk, Mr. Gideon."

Chapter Forty-One

"W-what are you doing—you can't be here!"

"Relax, Mister Three—or should I call you Mister Gideon, of the Three. Your partners are George Mathis and Ben Weaver." Those were the names Rick had given him for the Three.

"Jesus—" Gideon said, looking around to see who was watching them.

Clint also looked, but people seemed to be involved with their meals.

A waiter came over and Clint said, "I'll have what he's having. And put it on his bill."

"Yes, sir."

"Adams," Gideon said, "you're going to get me killed."

"I thought you were three men of business," Clint said. "Are you telling me you also deal in murder?"

"No, of course not—"

"Then why would you send me to Chinatown looking for a killer?" Clint asked.

"I was trying to help you clear Hartman," Gideon said.

"So tell me which of your partners hired someone to kill Ruth Bridges."

"That's not what we do," Gideon said.

"Then who does it?"

Gideon looked around again, sat back.

"Your steak's getting cold," Clint said. "You might as well keep eating."

Gideon sighed, picked up his fork and continued eating. The waiter came and put a plate of steak and vegetables in front of Clint.

"Come on, Gideon," Clint said. "Help me out, here."

"Everybody knows Chinamen kill people with knives," the man said.

"That's why you sent me to Chinatown?" Clint asked.

"I just thought—"

"Or did you send me there to get killed?" Clint went on. "Was that the plan of the Three?"

"We are individuals with many business interests, not killers," Gideon said. "We're not like Judge Wilkie."

"What about Wilkie?" Clint asked.

"He's the one framing Rick Hartman for the murder," Gideon said.

"So the judge had her killed to frame Rick?"

"We don't think so," Gideon said. "We think he's simply taking advantage of the murder, trying to pin it on Hartman to get rid of him."

"But why? What does he care about competition between saloons?"

"It's not that," Gideon said. "They're afraid that if Hartman runs for mayor, he'll win."

"Who's they?"

"The Judge and the Mayor."

"So they're in on the plan to frame Rick together, but they didn't have Ruth killed?"

"It doesn't seem likely."

"So they didn't kill Ruth, and your group didn't kill Ruth. Who does that leave?"

"A Chinaman," Gideon said, as if it made perfect sense.

"I think I'm going to have to talk to your two partners," Clint said.

"No, you can't!" Gideon said. "They can't know I met with you."

"Come on," Clint said, "you're telling me they didn't know about our meeting? That it wasn't planned?"

Gideon looked down at his plate.

"You're going to take me to meet them," Clint said, picking up his knife and fork, "right after we finish eating."

***

They found Mathis at one restaurant, and Weaver at another. Both men asked Gideon if he was crazy.

"It wasn't Gideon," Clint told them both. "It was me."

"Then let's go to our offices and talk," George Mathis said.

They all walked to the offices of The Three. Apparently, each man had his own, and there was another room they used for meetings. They took Clint in there.

"Have a seat, Mr. Adams," Mathis said.

They all sat at the long, mahogany meeting table, the Three on one side, and Clint on the other.

"What's on your mind, Mr. Adams?" Mathis asked.

"What do you call yourselves?" Clint asked.

"Why, we're the Three," Mathis said.

"No, I mean . . . Mr. Gideon told me he's called Three."

"I'm One," Mathis said, "and Mr. Weaver is Two."

"And do those numbers indicate who has the most influence?" Clint asked.

"They do," Mathis said.

"Then maybe you and me, we should talk alone," Clint suggested.

Mathis looked at his two partners and nodded. They both stood up and left the room.

"What's on your mind, Mr. Adams?"

Chapter Forty-Two

"I'm thinking the three of you wouldn't mind if Rick Hartman went to jail for murder," Clint said. "You'd probably buy his place."

"You've got that right," Mathis said. "But there's nothing criminal in that. It's just business."

"As long as you three had nothing to do with the killing," Clint said.

"Again," Mathis said, "that would be criminal, not business."

"So you're saying you don't do anything criminal?"

"We buy and sell."

"How much of the red light district do you own?" Clint asked.

"That's not important for you to know."

"And what about Chinatown?"

"Chinatown?" Mathis repeated. "Why would we want anything in Chinatown?"

"How about a Chinaman?" Clint asked. "With a blade?"

Mathis was a tall man with grey hair and a well groomed grey mustache. He smiled beneath it.

"You've been talking to Gideon," he said.

"What makes you say that?"

"Because he has this idea in his head that a Chinaman killed that woman, not Rick Hartman."

"You don't agree?"

Mathis shrugged.

"I don't have any theories," he said. "We're waiting to see how things turn out."

"And you'll be ready to swoop in and buy Rick's Place," Clint said.

"If it comes to that," Mathis said. "It's just business, Mr. Adams."

"Well, I'm going to find out who the real killer is. When I do, it better not be any of you, Mr. Mathis."

"You can call me One, if you like," Mathis said, with a grin.

"I don't think so," Clint said. "I believe in names, not numbers."

"It's not a number," Mathis said. "It's a position."

"How much longer do you think you'll be Number One, with Two and Three right behind you, waiting for you to fall?"

Mathis shook his head.

"They know their place, Mr. Adams," he said. "It's important for everyone to know their place."

"I'm getting the feeling this town is not my place, anymore," Clint said.

"Then you'll be leaving?"

"After I clear Rick Hartman of a murder charge," Clint said, "yes, and this time I won't be back."

"That's a shame," Mathis said. "This town is going to continue to grow."

Clint stood up and said, "That's what I'm afraid of."

He turned and walked out.

***

He had expected to see Two and Three in the hall after his talk with One, but they had apparently gone to their own offices, or home. Since he didn't feel the need to talk with either of them, he left the building.

Walking back toward Rick's Place he realized what a mess this whole matter was. There were so many people maneuvering to be on top as the town grew and grew, but none of them seemed to be murderers. They were business people and, as dirty as business could get, they weren't criminals.

He entered Rick's Place, got a beer from Shiloh at the bar and then carried it to Rick's table, where his friend was sitting with Ray Judd.

"You don't look happy," Judd said.

"I really don't like what's happened to this town," Clint said.

"Neither do I," Rick admitted.

174

Judd looked at Rick.

"Are you thinking of leaving?"

"If I close up shop and leave, that's what a lot of these people want me to do," Rick said.

"So what's your solution?" Clint asked.

"I could just set up in another town," Rick said, "but leave this place open, let somebody else run it."

"Well, from what I've been told," Clint said, "they're more afraid you'll run for mayor than anything else."

"I thought about it, just to tic them off, but no," Rick said, "I can't see myself being a politician."

"Maybe," Clint said, "if you told them that, and said you were leaving town, the charges against you would suddenly go away."

Rick gave Clint a concerned look.

"Even if that happened," he said, "I'd still have to find out who killed Ruth."

"I was afraid you were going to say that," Clint said.

Chapter Forty-Three

Judd left them, saying he was going back to his office to do some business.

"Now that he's gone," Clint said, "I have an idea."

"One you didn't want to talk about in front of Ray, obviously," Rick said.

"Well, he's an officer of the court, and was chosen for you by Judge Wilkie."

"So what's your idea?"

"Judge Wilkie," Clint said.

"What about him?"

"What if you and I went and talked to him tomorrow, told him your plans," Clint posed.

"And what would that accomplish?"

"Like I said before, maybe the charges would go away," Clint said.

"And like I said, I'd still want to find out who killed Ruth."

"But if you didn't have the murder charges hanging over your head, we'd have more time to do that, and we could start working on it together."

Rick thought about Clint's proposal for a few moments, then said, "It couldn't hurt."

"Tomorrow morning?"

"Why not?"

They had another drink, and then Clint went to his hotel for the night.

***

The next morning Clint met Rick outside of his place and they walked to the City Hall building together. The judge's clerk stared at them as they entered the office.

"We'd like to see the Judge," Clint said.

The clerk, Vincent, was staring at Rick with wide, watery eyes.

"Um, I—I'll check and see if the Judge has time."

Vincent stood and stumbled into the Judge's chambers, returned just moments later, leaving the door open.

"Judge Wilkie will see you."

Clint and Rick entered the chambers and closed the door behind them.

"You scared my clerk half to death," Judge Wilkie said. "He's not used to seeing murderers right in front of him."

"Accused murderer," Rick said.

"I stand corrected," Wilkie admitted.

"Seems to me he ought to get used to it, if he's going to keep being your clerk."

"And that's a good point," Wilkie said. "Why don't you gents have a seat and tell me what brings you here?"

"I think you have an idea why we're here, Judge," Clint said.

"And without your attorney," Wilkie said. "Why am I thinking this might be a threat rather than a bargain?"

"No threat," Clint said. "When this is over, Rick and I have the same intention."

"Which is?"

"To get out of town," Clint said.

"For good?"

"Exactly," Clint said.

Wilkie looked at Rick.

"That's your plan?"

"This town is changing too fast," Rick said. "It's time for me to move on."

"If," Clint added, "he's not convicted of murder."

"Ah," Wilkie said, "I see. You expected to tell me you're leaving town, and I'd drop the charges. I can't do that. There has to be a jury trial."

"Unless the real killer is revealed," Clint said.

"Well, yes . . . ." Wilkie said. "I'm sorry, but that's going to be what it takes."

Clint leaned forward.

"You know he didn't do it," he said. "That's why you gave him Ray Judd as a lawyer."

"Judd is competent," Wilkie said, "and he was available."

"You want me to get convicted, Wilkie," Rick said. "You never would've given me a lawyer you actually thought was competent."

"Well," Wilkie said, "he could be competent, if he applied himself a little more."

"Look," Clint said to Wilkie, "talk with your mayor. His job is in no danger from Rick. Drop the charges, and we'll leave town."

"You would close your establishment?" Wilkie asked Rick.

"No, I'll leave it open, being run by someone I trust," Rick said. "I don't have any desire to run for mayor."

"I'm impaneling a jury," Wilkie said. "We should be ready for you in two days. You have that long to find a killer. Any killer."

"We're going to find the right one," Clint assured him.

Chapter Forty-Four

Outside the City Hall building Rick said, "All right, so how do we find the real killer?"

"We've got two days," Clint said. "I'm supposed to meet with Chang tonight in Chinatown. Maybe we'll have the answer by then. If we don't, maybe he will."

"That's two maybes too many," Rick said. "What about Judd?"

"I'd like to keep from finding out just how competent he really is," Clint said. "That means keeping you out of court."

"Let's get a cup of coffee," Rick said, looking at a café across the street, "and you can tell me everyone you've talked to, so far."

Clint pointed and said, "Lead the way. The coffee's on you."

***

Over coffee and pie Clint told Rick about everyone he had spoken to so far, from the rancher Kellog, to the competition in the red light district, and Chinatown.

"Kellog and Crockett have nothing against me," Rick said.

"They both knew Ruth, but it's my opinion neither of them killed her."

"All right," Hartman said. "My competition in the red light district—Auggie Dewey and Father Elvis, I don't think they're capable of murder."

"Could they hire it done?"

Rick hesitated, then said, "No."

"What about Dean Macklin."

"Macklin could hire it," Rick said, "but why would he? He's convinced his place will eventually be more popular than mine."

"What about Chinatown?"

"There's no place in Chinatown who can compete with me or the red light district. They just cater to their own."

"Does that include Fong's?"

"Oh yeah," Rick said, "that's a dump. But Fong is happier there than he was back in China."

"You're not really helping to narrow this down any," Clint said. "What about the Three? They told me they work with business people, not criminals."

"Most business people—not including me, of course—*are* criminals," Rick said, "to one extent or another, but I don't think they're killers."

"What about Jack Snow?"

"He's a killer for hire," Rick said, "but not with a knife."

"Damn it, Rick," Clint said, "we're running out of options."

"You met Chang," Rick said. "He's capable of it."

"He said he didn't do it."

"You spoke to him for five minutes."

"I think I got to know him in that time," Clint said. "I'll learn more tonight."

"Let's hope you do," Rick said. "Otherwise I'm just going to have to depend on Ray Judd."

"And what do you think of him?"

"He's a lawyer," Rick said. "I trust them as much as I trust politicians."

"Well, he's *your* lawyer," Clint said, "so you're going to have to trust him."

"To a certain degree."

"In court," Clint said, "if and when you get there."

"I'm trusting you, my friend," Rick said, "to keep me out of court. After all, you got me out of jail."

Clint stood up.

"Well, you know that's not going to get done from here," he said.

Rick paid their bill and they left the café.

***

Clint walked Rick back to his saloon and told him he'd be better off staying there.

"You're going to see Chang in Chinatown, alone?" Rick asked.

"That's what I did last night," Clint said. "I'm just going to Fong's. I'm a regular customer there, now."

"Are you drinking his Baijiu?" Rick asked.

"What else has he got?"

"That stuff will make you go blind," Rick said. "Ask Fong for a Chinese beer. It's actually not bad."

"I'll do that," Clint said. "Thanks."

"And come back here when you're done," Rick said. "I'll give you a real drink and you can tell me what Chang had to say."

"You got a deal."

Rick went inside, and Clint started to walk down the street, with no definite goal in mind. He wondered when Jack Snow was going to put in an appearance. At least facing him would take up some time.

Chapter Forty-Five

There was one person Clint felt might be holding something back. He believed most of the people he had spoken to, but he couldn't read Lily, the girl running Ruth Bridges' shop. He decided to talk to her again before going to see Chang.

He walked to the shop, but found it closed. He tried the locked front door, but it wouldn't budge. When he knocked, nobody answered.

It was Clint's experience that back doors were rarely as secure as front ones, so he went around to the rear. When he tried that door, he found it as secure as the front. If he really wanted to get inside, he'd have to break a window. But if Lily wasn't present, there was no point.

He looked in the rear windows, then walked back around to the front and looked in the front. There was no sign of the girl, and he didn't know where she lived. Maybe he was wrong anyway. Maybe there was nothing she could do or say to help. He turned and walked away from the shop.

Clint decided to go to Chinatown early, and wait for Chang at Fong's.

***

"Baijiu?" Fong asked, as Clint stepped to the bar.

The Chinamen sitting at tables looked over at him and recognized him from his other visits. Not fearing that he would cause trouble, they went back to their drinks and conversation.

"No," Clint said, "I'd like to try some Chinese beer. I've been told it's pretty good."

"Yes," Fong said, "good."

He went to the other end of the bar, came back with a green bottle that had Chinese writing on it.

"*Tsingtao*," Fong said.

"That's the name of it?" Clint asked.

"Yes."

He tilted the bottle to his lips and sipped. The cold beer went down smooth.

"Have you seen Chang?" Clint asked.

"Not yet," Fong said, "he will be here soon. But he will not be able give you the killer you are looking for."

"Why not?"

Fong leaned forward and lowered his voice.

"The killer is his cousin," Chang said. "He will tell you he has nothing to tell you."

"But you're telling me."

"Yes."

"Why?"

"I like Chang," Fong said, "I do not like his cousin. He is . . . bad. He should . . . disappear."

"But Chang hires out to kill," Clint said. "Doesn't that make him bad?"

"Perhaps," Fong said, "but Chang is honorable. His cousin has no honor."

"And who's his cousin?" Clint asked.

Fong looked past Clint and said, "I will let him tell you."

Clint turned and saw Chang approaching the bar.

"I will have what Mr. Adams is having," Chang said to Fong.

The bartender put another bottle of beer on the bar. Chang picked it up and took a sip before speaking.

"I'm afraid I have bad news," he said. "But first . . . you did say you would pay me no matter what."

Clint took the money from his pocket and set it on the bar. "Same amount again," he said. "That was the deal."

Chang reached for the money, but Clint slapped his hand down over it.

"Give me the bad news," Clint said.

"I was unable to find the man you want."

"Is that a fact?"

"Yes."

Clint removed his hand from the money, allowing Chang to pick it up.

"What if I told you I know you're lying?" Clint asked.

"I would tell you," Chang said, "that the truth does not come cheap."

"What if it involved family?"

"Oh," Chang said, "for family it is even more expensive."

"Mr. Chang," Clint said, "I need to know who killed Ruth Bridges. I'm not leaving town until I do, and anyone who gets in my way will regret it." Clint put his hand on his gun to stress his point.

Chang had a knife on his belt. He put his hand on it, then moved it away. A knife, no matter how skilled the hand holding it was, would be no match for the Gunsmith.

"You don't want to be my enemy, Chang," Clint said.

Chang drank down his beer, waved at Fong for a second bottle.

"Chang?" Clint said.

"You will pay more?"

"I'll pay the same again," Clint said. "No more."

Chang stared at Clint until he took the money from his pocket and set it on the bar.

"My cousin," Chang said, picking up the money, "Ling."

"The waiter?"

Chang nodded.

"When he heard that I turned down the job," Chang said, "he took it."

"All right, then," Clint said. "There's one more question, and I'm not paying any extra for it."

"What is it?" Chang asked.

Clint leaned in and asked, "Who hired him?"

Chapter Forty-Six

Clint entered the Princess Pleasure Palace. The girl he recognized as Lisa stepped up to him.

"Can I help you, Mr. Adams?"

"I'd like to see Auggie," he said.

"Are you sure?" she asked, playing with her long hair in a flirty manner. "I could take you upstairs."

"I appreciate the offer, Lisa," Clint said, "but I need to see Auggie."

"Wait here, please," she said, dropping the flirtatious attitude. She turned and went off down the hall, only to return moments later. "Follow me, please."

She led him down the hall like before, but this time, instead of the room with the round table, she took him directly to Auggie's office.

"Thank you, Lisa," Auggie said, from behind her desk. "Go and take care of that other thing."

"Yes, Ma'am."

Lisa left, closing the office door behind her.

"Would you like to sit?"

"No, thanks," Clint said. "I need you to come with me, Auggie."

"Oh? Where? And why?"

"We're going to see Judge Wilkie."

"I've already struck him off, Clint," she said. "He's not welcome here."

"Well, I'm sure you'll be welcome at City Hall, especially once he learns that you hired a Chinaman to kill Ruth Bridges."

"And why would I do that?"

"Well, you hired it done because you didn't want to do it yourself," Clint said. "As for motive, it could have been personal or professional. I'm going to let somebody else figure out that part."

"And why would I go with you now?"

"Because if you don't," Clint said, "I'll shoot you."

She looked amused.

"You wouldn't."

"In the leg, or the arm," he went on, "no place vital, but it'll hurt. Your choice."

She hesitated a moment, then stood up. She was wearing a purple gown that showed a lot of cleavage. "I'd like to go to my room and change into something else."

"I'm sure the Judge won't mind," Clint said. "Besides, you might come out of your room with a new dress, and a gun,"

"You seem pretty sure of yourself, Clint," she said. "I'm not going to confess just because you take me to Judge Wilkie."

"You don't have to confess," Clint said. "We already have Ling in a jail cell."

"Ling?"

"The Chinaman you hired," Clint said. "He's already given us your name."

"Us?"

"The law."

Auggie frowned.

"Let's go."

Auggie looked at his gun

"I'm not going to march you out of here at gunpoint if you come willingly."

"That's very decent of you."

He opened the office door and she led the way to the front door. Some of the girls in the sitting room noticed and stared. There was no sign of Lisa, who was probably off taking care of that "other thing" Auggie had mentioned.

They left the building and Auggie hesitated right out front.

"Let's go," Clint said. "You know where the court building is."

"I'm just . . ." she started, looking around.

At that point a man came around from the side of the building and stood in front of them.

"Ah," Clint said, "I'm assuming Jack Snow was the 'other thing' you sent Lisa to do?"

"He was just upstairs with one of my girls," Auggie explained. "She didn't have far to go."

"And when did you hire him?" Clint asked.

"Soon after we talked," she said. "I convinced him to kill you for money, and not just for a reputation."

"So you offered to pay him."

"If and when the time came," Auggie said.

"Like now."

"Yes."

"Are you ready, Adams?" Jack Snow called.

"In a minute," Clint said, waving Snow away. "Auggie, why'd you have Ling kill Ruth?"

"Ruth used to be one of my girls," Auggie said, "another time in another town. We didn't part on good terms."

"So she had something on you that you didn't want anyone in this town to know. What was it?"

"I doesn't matter," Auggie said. "She's not going to tell."

"Adams!" Snow shouted. "I'm waitin'."

"He's getting impatient," Auggie told Clint.

"You stand off to the side and don't move," Clint said. "We're not done."

"We might be," she said.

"No," Clint said, "we're not."

Auggie took a few steps to the side to get out of the way. Some of the girls from inside crowded around the door and windows to watch.

Clint looked at Snow, who was standing relaxed. That was usually the sign of a man who was good with his gun.

"This is your play, Snow," Clint said. "Any time."

"I want to enjoy this moment," Snow said, with a smile. "It ain't every day a man—"

When Snow drew his gun in mid-sentence, it was no surprise to Clint. When they were ready, Snow started talking, as if he was in no hurry. That was a ploy, so that when he drew in mid-sentence Clint would be caught off guard.

Except that he wasn't. He didn't become the Gunsmith by being caught off guard.

He drew, beating Snow cleanly, before the man could even clear leather. And Snow was no amateur. His move was good, just not good enough. Clint's bullet hit him square in the chest, punching the air from his lungs, and the life from his eyes. It was a dead body that hit the ground.

Clint holstered his gun and looked at Auggie.

"Are you ready?"

Chapter Forty-Seven

"So she never confessed what her big secret was?" Rick asked.

It was the next day and Clint was sitting in his friend's saloon with both Rick and the lawyer, Judd.

"No," Clint said, "but Ling identified her as the person who paid him to kill Ruth."

"I guess we were lucky Chang decided to talk," Rick said.

"I made it worth his while," Clint said.

"Yes, you paid him, and didn't kill him," Judd said.

Clint sipped his beer.

"Well," Judd said, "Judge Wilkie has dropped the charges against you. So thanks to your friend, here, you're an innocent man."

"A *free* man," Clint corrected. "He was always innocent."

"So what are you fellas going to do now?" Judd asked.

"Clint's horse is right outside," Rick said, "so my guess is, he's leaving town."

"As soon as I finish this beer," Clint said.

"Will you be coming back any time soon?" Judd asked.

"This used to be a nice, quiet little town," Clint said. "It's not, anymore. So I think I'll have to find another nice quiet town where I can spend my leisure time."

"And you?" Judd asked Rick.

"I have a sour taste in my mouth," Rick said. "I'm going to have to see how long that lasts. Meantime, I'll start looking for a manager for this place, whether I stay or not."

"How about Shiloh?" Clint asked, looking over at the young bartender.

"He's on the list," Rick said.

"And if you left," Judd said, "where would you go?"

"It would be interesting to find a nice lazy town where I could buy a new place and build it up."

"Like this place?" Judd said.

"Better," Rick said. "There'd be no point in making a new place less than this."

Clint drained his mug and set it down.

"Time to go," Clint said.

All three men stood up, and Clint shook hands with Judd, then shared a warmer handshake with his friend, Rick.

"Stay in touch," Rick said, "so I can tell you where I am."

"I'll do that," Clint promised.

"Thanks, again, Clint," Rick said. "I owe you my life."

"It sounds trite," Clint said, "but that's what friends are for."

He turned, left Rick's place, mounted Eclipse, and rode out of Labyrinth, Texas for what he figured was the last time.

***

His intention was to ride north and put some good distance between himself and Labyrinth. However, that direction took him very near the Bar H. He decided to make a slight detour and see a man about a horse.

Coming August 27, 2020

THE GUNSMITH
462
The Gypsy King

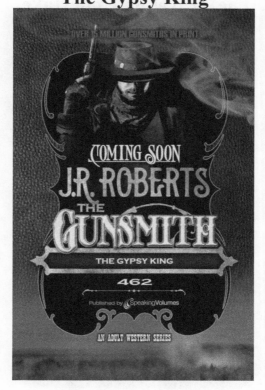

**For more information
visit:** SpeakingVolumes.us

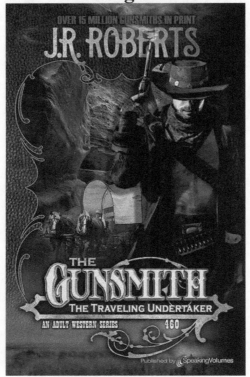

On Sale Now!

THE GUNSMITH *series*
Books 430 - 459
The Imperial Crown

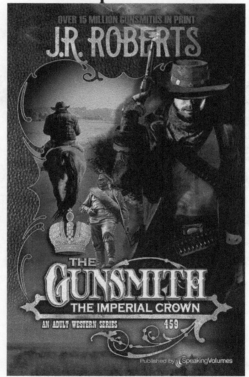

**For more information
visit:** SpeakingVolumes.us

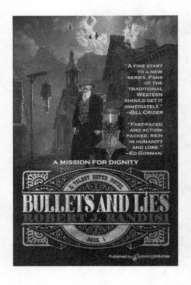 

Coming September 2020!

Lady Gunsmith
9
Roxy Doyle and the Lady Executioner

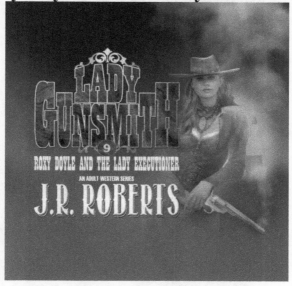

**For more information
visit:** SpeakingVolumes.us

On Sale Now!

**Lady Gunsmith
Books 1 - 8
Roxy Doyle and the Silver Queen**

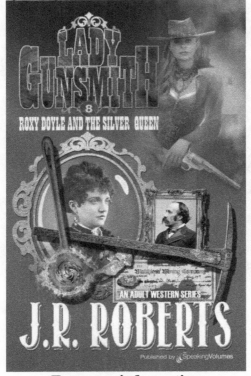

**For more information
visit:**

On Sale!

Award-Winning Author
Robert J. Randisi (J.R. Roberts)

For more information
visit: www.SpeakingVolumes.us

CPSIA information can be obtained
at www.ICGtesting.com
Printed in the USA
LVHW111926050922
727604LV00018B/256